SHADOW SWORD

BLUESHADE BOOK 2

CLAY BALL

This book is dedicated to my great-aunt
Patricia Fussell.
Thanks for putting me
on the high school drumline, Aunt Pat.

~

Other books by Clay Ball

Blueshade series
Shattered Creation
Shadow Sword

...and this is only the beginning.

Pronunciation Guide

Hurr: Her
Protex: Protects
Cair: Care
Enérgeia: In-er-gay-uh
Kynd: Kind
Incurajuh: In-cuh-ra-juh
Licemah: Lih-cih-muh
Securitie: Sec-yur-i-tee
Kumpashin: Compassion
Gentull: Gentle
Deefins: Defense
Kunsiderut: Considerate
Kunsern: Concern
Blueshade: Blue-shade
Yarl: Yar-ull
Zanesu: Za-ne-zu
Raliga: Ra-li-ga
Bacaniber: Buh-can-i-ber
Tenderr: Tender
Tideicthy: Tide-ik-thee
Aidaria: A-dar-ee-uh
Sheeld: Shield

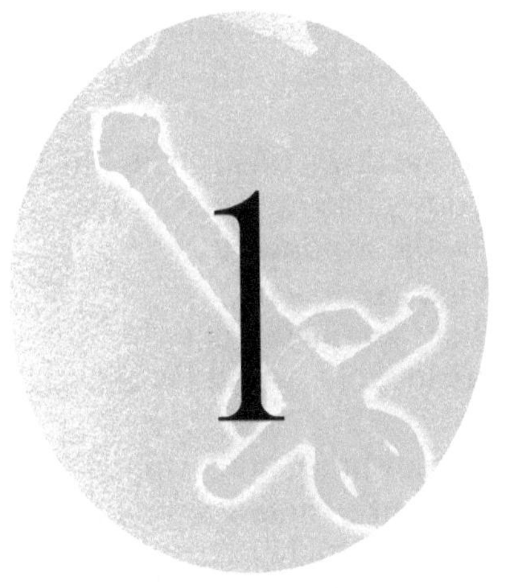

THORN IN THE FLESH

Hurr paced the length of his quarters. The soft, cotton blanket lay crumpled at the foot of his bed and the afternoon sun bathed the table in golden light.

There was a knock on the stone doorway. Hurr paused in his pacing.

"Protex," he said. The red-haired angel tucked a small piece of pink fruit into his white robe.

"Hello, Hurr," Protex replied and entered the room. "Just got back from Yarl Island. Fixed the windows on the Cathedral."

Hurr stepped out of the sunlight. "I see they've given you more tokens of gratitude."

"I've a good-sized collection now. Running out of room on my desk. How 'bout you? Get your toxitrike horn yet?"

Hurr sat down on his bed. "In a way."

Shadows flickered across the walls as three birds flew by the windowsill.

"What happened?"

"There was an accident."

Hurr looked up and Protex saw sadness in his eyes.

"I had my horn, but I tripped. The poisoned tip went into Cair's shoulder. Praise the Voice that Zafe was there to heal her."

"'S a good thing, right?"

"Of course, Protex! But I keep playing it over and over again in my head. I caused *harm* to one I love."

While Hurr sat in silence, Protex's eyes roamed the room. He saw a single white feather on the wall next to the window. Some enérgeia probably held it there.

"Cair give you that feather?"

"How did you know?"

"Got one of Kynd's feathers in my room. 'S special to me."

"I feel the same way about Cair. I only wish I could've saved her from that poison."

"Maybe y'can. Save her, I mean."

"Do you think there's a way?"

Protex sat down next to Hurr. "We're angels, y'know. *Angels.* We can fly and use enérgeia to manipulate matter. We use our powers for the Voice. But what if we used them for ourselves?"

Protex jerked his hand and a yellow ball of swirling enérgeia appeared in it.

"Remember when those mountain goats were caught in that rock slide?" Protex continued.

"The ones near the lake that Incurajuh healed?"

"What if she didn't have to? What if we made sure there wasn't a rock slide at all?"

Hurr stroked his chin. "That sounds like *control*. If we could eat spirit fruit, I'd think you'd been eating the Self-Control fruit. Isn't it pink?"

"'S green," Protex pulled the pink fruit from his robe. "'S the Love fruit. What they give me for fixing the windows. Twenty-second piece. Or twenty-third? Lose count sometimes."

Hurr walked over to the windowsill and caressed the feather.

"This control we're talking about...can it work? Won't the Voice know if we try?"

"Probably." Protex rolled the fruit between his thumb and finger. "Trick'll be taking a little bit at a time. *Slowly. Gradually.* Before y'know it, you'll have extra time to do things y'want."

"And I'll spend that extra time making sure nothing hurts Cair ever again," Hurr said. He gazed wistfully at the white feather and a slow smile spread across his face.

The fruit between Protex's fingers popped. "She'd like that."

Behind Hurr's back, Protex narrowed his eyes.

"Wouldn't you, Cair?"

SPRUCE TREE

Protex sounded like he was right there beside me. I almost fell from the tree branch I was sitting in. My hands grabbed the rough bark. I felt dizzy from the vision and it took a few seconds to adjust to the pines and spruces around me. The forest rolled like a green wave to the mountain peaks far above. The misty river roared as it tumbled off the cliff, spilled past the plateau and emptied into the basin beneath it. Protex wasn't here. He disappeared last night during the battle.

It was the first day of early-Spring. My hands relaxed and I shifted my position in the spruce tree. From the spruce tree, I could see what had once been my home. Some buildings still stood, untouched by the Battle of Licemah. Others had been reduced to piles of rubble.

Memories of the fight flashed through my mind. The hallway where Protex had trapped Securitie. The cliff where the Green Giant had thrown Laff to his death. The rushing river below where I'd seen the hatred in Sage's eyes.

Every now and then, an angel would fly into the city and back out again. The Voice had probably given them tasks. I hadn't had any yet, which was fine with me. My quiet spot in the spruce tree was a welcome change from the frenzied fighting of last night.

"Oh, Ca-yair!"

Securitie was standing at the foot of my tree, her hand shielding her eyes against the sunlight.

"Are you okay? You've been up there all morning."

"I'm fine."

"Can you come down? I thought you might want to help me get Jolene."

"Where'd you hide her again?"

"Across the savannah. Hey, hold on!"

Before I knew it, she was hovering there in front of me. The wind pulled on her red, curly locks.

"Maybe I'm wrong, but I get the feeling you don't want to come with me. Are you *sure* you're okay?"

I shifted my body away from her. "I'm fine."

"You can talk to me if you're not..."

"Sec..."

"...or at least talk to the Voice..."

"Sec, that's enough!"

I stood up suddenly and unfolded my wings.

"Many angels died last night!" I yelled at her. "I don't want to go anywhere! Leave me alone!"

Securitie's eyes widened and her lower lip trembled.

"Well, if that's what you w-want..."

She disappeared over the treetops.

THE RUINS OF
LICEMAH

A few hours later, I returned to Licemah. Stone and debris littered the streets. Smashed benches and learning boards lay scattered outside the learning hall. Angels flitted in and out of the ruins, looking for lost weapons or scrolls or potion bottles. Several were shrouded in yellow light as they used enérgeia to lift dead bodies of their attackers-wolves, bats and even some dragons. Then, the dead were thrown into the basin below.

I made my way through the ruins. Several angels looked like they might need help, but I didn't go to them. My mind was a whirl of images and scattered voices. Only the impact of running into someone brought me back to reality.

The other angel picked himself off the ground. He was gathering the dropped weapons back into his burlap sack.

"Sorry," I mumbled as I bent down to help him. I handed him some broken arrows and a silver knife. My hands froze over a familiar sword. Two snakes crisscrossed over the bronze hilt.

"I'll take that," the angel said. His hand closed over the hilt and he carefully slid it into his sack. I examined him closely. His windswept blonde hair. His blue eyes. It was Kumpashin, one of the angels who'd fought the dragons with me. He stood up abruptly.

"Kumpashin," I said and stood up, too. "You know that's Hurrikiller's sword, right?"

He hefted the sack over his shoulder. "Yep. Gard's having me collect every weapon in the city. If they belonged to a demon, he'll destroy them."

"Good. Make sure you get them all."

Kumpashin gave me a brief smile. He walked away with the burlap sack dangling behind him. I watched him disappear around the corner of the Temple. Then, I resumed my wandering.

My feet carried me to a monument near the quarters. The Voice had built it this morning; one tall angel surrounded by three smaller angels. The tall angel's wide arms embraced the smaller ones who gathered into his chest. These three little ones had half-closed eyes and serene smiles. The tall one gazed on them with understanding as he sheltered them protectively. It reminded me of a father lion and his cubs. Bronze coated the monument, giving it a soft, glowing appearance.

"Cair?"

I knew Gard was standing right next to me.

"What a fitting tribute this monument is," he said when I didn't answer. "Honoring the ones who lost their lives in the War of the Fallen. They are at peace now and dwell in God's Country."

In my head, I saw Hurrikiller blasting Gard off the Temple roof with dark enérgeia. How was Gard acting so calm now?

"I have some tasks to do. Would you mind accompanying me? It will do you good to stretch your wings."

The image was replaced by Sage screaming as the wind blew her away from me.

"Where are you going?"

This time, he was silent. I huffed in irritation and turned around. Gard stood there with a satchel over his shoulder.

"Your blue sash is gone."

He inclined his head. "Indeed. I wore it as a symbol of rank during the War of the Fallen. Now that the war is over, I no longer have need of it. Kumpashin has informed me that the eight surviving demons have fled the Mainland. Some are on the Tip, while others are on the Peninsula. They will be watching us, waiting for our next move."

"And what *is* our next move, exactly?"

Gard chuckled and slapped his satchel. "Our next move, my sister, *is* to follow the sun!"

PROPHECY OF THE THREE

The wide savannah used to cover a third of the Mainland. I'd spend a whole day just running through the tall grass, racing the herds of grassgallis and woodparas.

But, of course, those were the days before the war.

Now, half of the savannah was covered by an enormous swamp. Murky water surrounded the low-hanging trees. The air lay thick and heavy; fog draped across cypresses and mangroves. Sunlight barely made it past the canopy.

We took care to fly above the tree line. Eventually, the trees thinned out and the swamp opened into a large clearing. Ruins of a castle rested on the wet ground. A wooden drawbridge with busted chains lay on its side. One of the towers had collapsed. Chunks of the battlement had fallen into a sickly green pond and the ends of a raised portcullis stuck out from the bottom of an arch like teeth. We landed by that arch.

"This used to be Liberag," Gard said. "The demons' first base of operations. This is the spot they fled to when the Voice cast them out."

There was a crack as a branch broke off a nearby tree. It landed in the murky water with a splash. Gard's hand gripped the hilt of his sword. Yellow swirls of light formed in my left palm. For minutes we waited, ears strained, eyes sweeping the trees for any movement. Eventually, Gard relaxed his shoulders. He removed his hand from his hilt. I felt the enérgeia leave me as I lowered my palm.

"Perhaps the tree is dying," Gard said to me. "Or we frightened a squirrel."

"Must've been one big squirrel."

After we crossed under the portcullis, we found ourselves in a courtyard. Stone bricks littered the path that led up to the keep. Dozens of four-clawed footprints were etched in the dirt. Another image flashed through my mind: a red, scaly creature with wings blasting me with a vortex of flames.

"Dragons?"

"Not at the moment," Gard said. "The sole inhabitant of this lonely place is quite occupied."

Gard pointed towards the right wall. A wolf was frozen in place on a gray pedestal. The six-foot tall beast crouched low, as if it prepared to spring. Thick black fur covered the massive body. The yellow eyes stared straight ahead; the wolf didn't even know we were there. Gard tapped on its back with his sword. A metallic *clang* sounded, but the animal didn't move.

"Have you seen him before, Cair?"

I shook my head.

"This is the Wolf Lord," Gard continued. "He led the packs that chose to serve Hurrikiller. Hurrikiller increased his size for that allegiance. Are you sure you haven't seen him?"

I shrugged. "Between giants, dragons and everything else, I'm pretty sure I missed him."

Gard glanced up at the fog swirling around the treetops. "In the battle, the Wolf Lord tried to attack the Voice. Then the Voice turned him to stone and put him here. Perhaps this will be his home until the end of time. But the Wolf Lord is not why we came. Let us leave this place."

We glided through the swamp and zigzagged around trees that grew from the slimy water. Fish darted in the shallows as egrets and storks hunted them. Frogs and crickets sang their own songs. Monkeys hooted and hollered as they chased each other through the trees. It was as if the entire swamp affirmed the Voice still had control, even in the wake of Hurrikiller's violence.

We stopped at a smaller clearing, one with a large gray rock in the center. I could probably sit on it if I wanted to. Gard ran his hand across the smooth surface and whispered some words. The rock glowed faintly with light. Part of the top opened like a mouth, revealing a four-foot-long empty space. Gard unbuckled his satchel and pulled out something yellow. I remembered seeing it in the forge, twenty-four years ago.

"Gentull made that, didn't he?"

Gard nodded. The yellow object was part metal, part glass. The letters N, S, E, W and C were etched in different spots. Under each letter was an empty slot, big enough to hold something inside. Gard placed this object inside the rock's empty space, causing the top to slide back into place. It was a large, gray rock once more. Gard turned to me.

"Remember last night when we briefly discussed *prophecy*? As promised, I will tell you more."

He opened the satchel again. There were two scrolls, a regular one and a black one with a blood-red seal. Gard handed me the regular one and I unrolled it. Sentences were arranged in rows, made by Gard's elegant handwriting:

The dark angel comes to call, bringing desperate cries,
Judgement from on high shall fall, three times he will die,
Time the first by a brother, time the second by another,
Time the third by a white-hearted child,
But resurrected he shall be,
Time the first by dragon knife, time the second by king's wife,
Time the third, the Voice will not allow his return to life

Then, at the bottom, in bolder letters:

PROPHECY OF THE THREE

I handed the scroll back to Gard. "Prophecy of the Three?"

"That is the name I call it. It refers to three deaths."

"Why would someone need to die *three* times? It sounds horrible!"

Gard gave me a sideways look. "If someone had committed evil in their first life, would you say they could find redemption in their second or third?"

He knew I was thinking about Hurrikiller. His expression softened.

"Hope is a fragile thing, Cair. It can be snatched away in an instant. I would not give you any unless I was absolutely sure the prophecy is specific."

"What makes you think it's about Hurrikiller?"

"*Time the first, by a brother*," he quoted. "That brother could be me. Or Zafe, since that is the name of my sword."

I felt a lump in my throat. "So, you're saying he'll be back?"

"If he does come back, then he might be redeemed by the Voice. And then, who knows? Maybe the other demons will be redeemed, too."

"After all this?" I jabbed a pointed finger at the swamp. "Why would the Voice forgive *him*?"

"Cair, as much as I agree with you, I cannot put an absolute over the future. Prophecies will happen, because the Voice..."

"Hurr broke my heart!" I yelled. The monkeys in their trees fell silent.

"You need to forgive him, Cair," Gard whispered. "Not for his sake, but for yours. Let the Voice's love heal your broken heart."

"Bor-ing!"

A demon sat on one of the tree branches. Bumps covered his skin and made the sneer on his face more hideous. Gard's hand moved to the hilt of his sword. My hand started glowing with enérgeia.

"You really think you'll hurt me with *those* things?" the demon asked, yawning.

"Why are you here, Deefins?" Gard's voice shook with anger.

The demon swung his legs idly. "I'm here to tell Cair that Hurrikiller didn't really love her."

I screamed and threw a blast of enérgeia at him. It cut the branch from the tree and sent it crashing into the bushes below. Deefins only leaped up onto the next one, grinning.

Gard looked at me with warning in his eyes. "Cair, he is trying..."

"*Trying* to anger me?" I interrupted and formed another yellow ball.

Deefins scratched his chin. "Come to think of it, he *did* spend a lot of time with Sage. Maybe he loved *her* instead of a goody-goody bird-wing like *you*."

I unfurled my wings, ready to fly up at Deefins and blast every part of him that I could reach. Suddenly, my whole body froze. I couldn't move! Gard walked in front of me and pulled a piece of green fruit from his satchel.

"Forgive me, Cair, but you need this," Gard said and stuffed it into my mouth. The fruit dissolved before I could taste it. But a cool feeling of calm and restraint came over me. My anger subsided like sand washed out to sea. I could move again. Gard watched me carefully.

"Sorry," I said and shook my head. "I thought you said spirit fruit wouldn't work on angels?"

"I did not think it would. But when I fed you the Self-Control fruit..."

"Bor-ing!"

Scaly, bat-like wings extended from Deefins' back.

"Oh, well. I got what I needed. See you around, *bird-wings*."

Deefins took off above the trees. Gard's satchel snapped shut.

"After him!"

We flew over the tree line, trying to catch up with Deefins. The demon stayed maybe fifty feet ahead of us. Whenever we'd get close, he'd speed up.

The satchel bounced against Gard's chest. A look of concentration spread across his face and he opened his hands. Balls of yellow light shot from them as he tried to knock Deefins from the sky. I sent enérgeia from my hands, too. Deefins suddenly dropped thirty feet. One of his wings had a small tear in it. We closed the distance quickly. Soon, we'd be able to...

Pain in my legs. Falling towards an old oak tree...

Then nothing.

5

MY EVERYTHING

Three angels huddled over a table near the back of the library. Rays of afternoon light filtered through the windows.

"And *then* she said I should talk to the Voice!" Hurr raged and slammed his fist down on the table.

"Why would you?" Protex asked. He leaned back in his chair.

"Yeah, why would you?" Kynd echoed. "All you did was ask a question!"

"A *reasonable* question!" Hurr continued, rolling his eyes. "*'Until then, seek the repentance you need'.* After that, Sage and I flew away from class."

Protex glanced around the room. Dozens of scrolls had been stacked neatly on the shelves.

"Where's she now?"

The three angels leaned forward.

"She's looking," Hurr whispered. "Looking for a new place. This control stuff we've been doing, it's not going to go unnoticed for much longer. We need a place to be able to do what we want."

Protex nodded with approval, but Kynd gasped.

"Leave Licemah? What about the buildings? Can't exactly pack 'em up."

Protex's hand found hers under the table. "Relax, Kynd. 'S got a plan for that."

"The forge," Hurr said. "I want you two to take some building materials from there. Some wood, hammers, ingots..." Red flames danced around his fingers. "Our enérgeia can make the fire we need. And *then,* we kill the Spotless Flock."

Kynd's eyes widened as Hurr went on. "Gard once said that the Spotless Flock has power in their blood. But he never said what *kind* of power. What if this power makes us stronger than the Voice? The world would be ours. And *she'd* see how right I am."

He stood. "Grab the materials. Meet me in the savannah at dusk."

The two other angels bowed and Hurr left them. Kynd waited for Hurr to climb up the stone steps to the library entrance. Then, she turned to Protex.

"I like this plan, Protex. But if we rebel against the Voice, d'you think Hurr will be our new leader?"

"'S already got the nerve. Just wish he'd stop trying to convince Cair that he's right."

Kynd smirked. "You think he likes *her*? Can't he see how *big* her freckles are?"

"'S got one of her feathers in his quarters."

"Really?"

"If she's who he wants, we can't change his mind. Just like you're the one I want."

The two moved closer together. Kynd stroked Protex's cheek with her palm while he kissed her forehead. She giggled.

"I like you, too, Protex. More than any other angel. More than the Voice, even."

Protex played with her blonde hair. "My sweet, you're my *everything*."

Time stood still. Kynd was as rigid as a statue, her lazy smile frozen on her face. Protex gazed at her longingly. Then his eyes narrowed.

"*There* you are, Cair. Have a seat."

I was frozen, too, in the same seat Hurr had been sitting in.

How did I get here? What was going on?

"In the Swamp, are you?" Protex continued. "When Hurrikiller made the Shadows, he cursed that part of the savannah. Turned it into a swamp. Yeah, that bit wasn't fun. 'S hard to see Shadows in the dark. They ate Mursee and Nerture before he could control them."

My hands couldn't open. Every inch of me was still. My eyes could only stare straight ahead.

"See, Cair, when the giants blasted you on that bridge, you should've died. But it worked out, didn't it? You're still alive, and I get to mess with your mind whenever I want."

Protex's skin blistered until the smoothness of it had been replaced with rough bumps. His white robe darkened to black and scaly wings emerged from his back. Twin horns burst through his red hair.

"Why'd you do it? Why'd you kill her, Cair?"

The images rushed through my mind. Stone stairways collapsing. Wolves howling in the night. Securitie struggling helplessly in midair while Kynd advanced. The three-pointed sai in Kynd's hand. Me yanking her from the floor and plunging her own weapon into her robe. Feeling her body go limp.

The library came back into focus. I was still bound to the chair. Protex sat on the table inches away.

"She even begged for mercy," he hissed. "You didn't even give her *that*."

He reached inside his robe and pulled out something small and black. He smeared it across my face.

"'S used to be the Love fruit. But now, 's the *Hate* fruit. Hate's all I got for you, Cair."

His claws dug into the table.

"And I'm just getting started."

A KINGDOM
DIVIDED

"Gard and Cair captured! Wait 'til he finds out!"

"Reward us, he will! Rise in the ranks, says I!"

The sound of cackling voices brought me back from the vision. There was a tight pressure across my chest and arms. Chirps of insects and croaks of bullfrogs. The air was heavy with a rotten, unpleasant smell. Fog drifted across the damp grass and the shadows were slowly darkening.

The swamp. Not the library. I was tied to a large cypress tree. Gard was bound next to me by the same black rope. He stared at our captors with disgust.

Two demons hopped around a small fire. Both wore tattered black robes. The taller one had a long nose, almost like a snout. The shorter one had tiny horns just visible over matted black hair. They both hopped from one foot to the other and clapped their hands. Gard's satchel and sword lay under a clump of fronds not far away.

"Now, Friend'll be back at the bottom, says I!" the shorter one whooped.

The taller one stopped hopping and glanced at his companion. "Let's not forget it was *me* who brought them down, Kunsiderut."

Kunsiderut stopped hopping, too. "But *I's* the one who saw them, 'member? Who followed them from Liberag? *Me*, says I."

The demons glared at each other. I felt Gard nudge me with his shoulder. He rolled his eyes at the two demons.

"Kunsern and Kunsiderut," he called loudly. "Of course, it would be you two."

Kunsern's long snout broke out in a toothy grin. "Glad to see you're awake. How'd you like the..."

"Hold on, says I!"

Kunsiderut pushed past him.

"What you mean, eh? '*Of course, it would be you two*'. You being funny?"

When Gard didn't answer, the demon drew back his fist and punched him in the face. A red bruise formed on his right cheek. I tried to lift my arms, but the black rope held them tight.

"No one gives us any respect, says I," Kunsiderut snorted and stomped away. "That'll change when we bring you to Protex."

He grabbed Gard's satchel and shook it hard. The two scrolls fell out. Three white lily petals also fluttered to the moist ground.

"Leave those alone!" Gard yelled. The bruise on his face began to turn purple.

"Those things must be *special,*" Kunsern said. "But it's the *sword* I want." He picked up Gard's sword and examined it with interest.

"The sword that killed Hurrikiller?" Kunsiderut tossed the satchel aside. "It's *mine,* says I."

Kunsern glared at the shorter demon. "You want credit for bringing in these two bird-wings? Fine, but only if *I* keep the sword."

"*Bor-ing!* What if *I* take the sword and the two bird-wings and get the credit myself?"

Deefins glided down from the canopy. He landed on the other side of the fire and retracted his wings. A three-pronged trident was in his hands.

Kunsern raised the sword and gnashed his teeth together. Kunsiderut hissed and crouched down low as if he was getting ready to jump. Deefins only laughed and tossed the trident back and forth from hand to hand.

"Kunsern and Kunsiderut? Of course, it'd be you two!"

Kunsiderut growled and flung himself at Deefins. Deefins stepped to the side and smacked the short demon with the butt of his weapon. Kunsiderut howled as he was sent flying into a hardwood tree.

"I'd rather it was you two than Protex or Friend," Deefins continued as Kunsern stalked towards him with the sword held high. "How many bird-wings did you *kill* at Licemah? Oh, sorry. I meant, *injure.* How many bird-wings did you *injure* at Licemah?"

Kunsern stabbed forward, but Deefins blocked it easily. He swept the trident across the ground. Kunsern fell flat on his back and the sword landed in a murky puddle.

"Not even one? I killed *many*. I even roughed one up before the Shadows got to him. The big one who used to work in the forge."

My throat tightened.

"Gentull?" I sputtered. "You mean Gentull?"

Deefins's eyes glittered. "The big one who yells, *'oi!'* all the time? Yeah, Sage *loves* her prisoner. Just think what she'll say when I bring her two more!"

Kunsiderut picked himself off the ground and pounced forward again. Deefins swung his trident easily, and made Kunsiderut trip and fall on top of Kunsern. The two demons moaned in pain.

"Poor Kunsern and Kunsiderut! And Friend, too! You three *really* think Protex can be our leader? Nah. Me, Sheeld and Hartee think Sage will. She was closer to Hurrikiller than your redhead *ever* was."

An enormous tremor rocked the swamp. Several branches broke off their trees and landed all around us. Water in the puddles rippled and leaves fluttered from above. The chorus of frogs and insects changed into an alarm. Other unseen animals added their cries of panic; we heard them crashing through the undergrowth, fleeing whatever was heading this way.

Deefins narrowed his eyes as he scanned the foliage. While his head was turned, the other two demons scrambled off the ground, their eyes wide with terror.

"Sage can have 'em, says I!" Kunsiderut moaned.

"We're out of here!" Kunsern yelled.

Both demons tripped over each other as they crashed through the vegetation and disappeared into the swamp. Directly in front of us, dozens of trees cracked as a gigantic silhouette loomed out of the fog. Deefins took a step back as he gazed up at the massive form.

It was the largest bird I'd ever seen. The golden body nearly blinded me in contrast to the dark swamp and it had talons the size of trees. The bird opened its beak and trilled. Being so big, the trill sounded like a roar. It opened its wings and we turned our heads as strong winds blasted our faces. The bird stood defiant as it towered over the swamp.

Deefins gave up shielding his eyes and lunged forward. He buried his trident in the middle claw on the left talon. Another screech shook the world and the bird's head came down. Deefins leaped away as an eight-foot beak jabbed into the ground. The bird raised its head and I could see that one of its golden eyes was the size of an angel.

"Whoa, *you're* a big bird!" Deefins spun his hands together. "But you'll die just like other ones!"

The black enérgeia shot from his hands. Before it could hit the bird, a shower of white snow fell upon it. The enérgeia shuddered and transformed into seven, small black birds. Deefins stared at them.

An angel landed next to the bird's talon. She shook her curly red hair out of her face as she closed her satchel. She waved cheerfully at the demon.

"Hi, Deefins! You know Dad doesn't like you messing with His animals. Go get him, birdies!"

The birds chirped eagerly as they flew toward Deefins. He growled and smacked the first one into a rock. But the bird only bounced off and came at him again. The other six were circling him and pecking all the parts they could reach. Deefins stumbled deeper into the swamp with the black birds hovering around him. The undergrowth soon swallowed them up.

With a loud *snap!* the black rope vanished. The angel was right there, shadowed against the bird's glowing body. She slipped the potion bottle back into her satchel.

"Sec?" I asked as she helped me up. "How'd you find us?"

"Well, I just got Jolene from the savannah..."

"*That's* Jolene?"

Securitie put a hand to her mouth. "Yikes, I almost forgot!"

She pulled another potion bottle out of her satchel and threw it hard. It burst on the bird's talon and golden smoke covered the whole animal. The smoke swirled for a few seconds before disappearing. There was a startled shriek from above and Jolene the alicanto glided down to rest on Securitie's shoulder. She ruffled her feathers as Securitie fed her a golden bar.

I pulled Gard to his feet. The bruise on his face was fading.

"Praise the Voice I got here when I did," Securitie said. "The enérgeia in that rope would've turned your face into stone!"

Gard rubbed the side of his face where Kunsiderut had hit him. "Praise the Voice indeed. Ah, for the Enlarging potion, did you have to amplify the base line of a quaketitan?"

"Yeah," Securitie answered. "I thought about amplifying a mountain instead, but you know..."

"Mountains are non-living. Your potion was successful nonetheless. And thank *you*," Gard added, bowing to Jolene. "The Mighty Bird of Blueshade, Scarer of Demons."

Jolene swallowed the rest of the bar and chirped contentedly.

"Hey, Sec," I said, making sure she looked right at me. "I need to apologize to you."

"Oh, Cair, you don't have to..."

"Yes, I do. For snapping at you this morning. The fight last night really shook me up. I'm tired, confused, sad and sometime*s* I don't know *how* I feel."

Jolene squawked as Securitie came forward and wrapped her arms around me. "I forgive you, Cair! You're still my friend!"

Gratitude settled inside of me and drowned out those awful whispers as I returned the embrace. I saw Gard smile at me.

"What?"

He chuckled. "This day is filled with good news. You have forgiveness. And we have learned that Gentull is indeed alive."

"He is?" Securitie exclaimed and broke away from me.

We caught her up on what the demons had told us. Gard paced back and forth.

"Without Hurrikiller, the demons are a kingdom divided," he muttered under his breath.

"...Sage has Gentull imprisoned...but we need to know *where*...ah, I have it!"

He turned to Securitie. "I need you to find Foster. Tell him we are in need of some Tracking enérgeia. As for the Object, any tool in the Forge will do."

She nodded eagerly. "I'm on it!"

Securitie's wings unfolded. She whistled and held open her satchel. Jolene flew into it. Once the alicanto was snugly tucked in, Securitie took off into the sky. Gard crouched on the marshy ground and carefully picked up the three flower petals Kunsiderut had dumped out. He gazed at them fondly and placed them back in his satchel. He also gathered up the two scrolls and slid his sword back into his sheath.

"We have one more stop."

LAST OF THE YARL

Life began again on Yarl Island, too. Pines and oaks covered the places where crops of spirit fruit used to be. Foxes scampered across the forest floor and woododos hid from them by using camouflage to blend in with the tree trunks. We flew toward the mountain that towered over the east side of the island. The staircase that ringed the mountainside was gone and the path to the top looked lonelier without it.

We landed on the summit. Up here, seven or eight charred yarl houses remained. The cathedral remained firmly planted. Light sparkled on the green and yellow stained-glass windows. Gard walked up to the cathedral wall. He ran his hand over the foundation, finally stopping at the southwest corner. He pulled the black scroll from his bag. Gard swung his arm forward and yellow light flashed. When I looked over his shoulder, I saw the scroll firmly set in the foundation.

Gard shook his hand. "Quite an impact, but it will do."

"Why'd you put it there?"

"I do not know."

"*You don't know?*"

He only chuckled, like what I said was amusing.

"Come now, Cair, we've been here before. The Voice tells us the *what* without telling us the *why*. I know my purpose is to serve the Voice and His designs. Whatever the reason, this scroll is part of the foundation now."

Before I could say more, I heard slow, shuffling footsteps behind us. It was a yarl. His legless feet carried his potato-like body towards us. Ragged breathing came from the vast mouth stretched across his stomach. A long gash ran across the top of his bald head.

"Hello, Oattop," Gard said, bowing.

"Brother Gard," the yarl replied in his deep, slow voice. He blinked his brown, earthen eyes. "Are you here to take me home?"

"I am."

Oattop exhaled and gently touched the wound on his head. I had a sudden flashback of giant bats dropping yarl to their deaths.

"Ah, angels, I am ready for...*God's Country*."

Oattop closed his eyes, as if he could see a place other than Yarl Mountain. I glanced at Gard. He gave me a knowing smile, which confirmed it. Yarl souls could go to God's Country, just like ours. Oattop was dying.

With his eyes still closed, Oattop began to rock back and forth. He hummed a rustic melody, one unfamiliar to my ears. Then he fell backwards. His potato body landed in the grass. He rolled over to his left side and his head eyes locked on the setting sun. A flock of seagulls glided over the beach below.

Gard knelt down next to Oattop's body. "What do you see?"

"Light..." the yarl whispered faintly. "...light and...castle in the sky..."

My thoughts were still on that day when the bats had invaded this island. Hundreds of yarl were slaughtered. Each shallow breath of Oattop reminded me of them. Reminded me of how fragile life really was.

"Is there a gate around the castle?" Gard prompted.

"Yes...the white gate opens..."

"Now what do you see?"

The corners of Oattop's mouth twitched. *"...my family...and...friends...open...arms..."*

The last breath left his mouth and his eyes closed forever.

We buried the last yarl on the beach below and stacked dozens of seashells on top of his grave. Waves lapped against the shore as the sun dipped below the horizon. The night wind blew my hair against my face as I stood with my arms crossed. Gard closed his eyes as he sang the lament over the mound of seashells. A few woododos listened from their tree trunks, their small, fat bodies camouflaged against the bark. When Gard was done, the dinosaurs waddled back into the shadows.

"And that concludes our errands for today," Gard said at last. "Thank you for joining me."

"Is it true what you told him? That yarl souls can go to God's Country?"

"Yes. Are you surprised?"

I shook the sand from my left sandal. "I thought it was only for angels."

"We are not the only children the Voice has made," Gard replied. "God's Country is a place of everlasting peace and rest. Who are we to say who is and isn't allowed? I long for it, though I have never seen it. I have many tasks to finish before that day comes."

The clouds thickened as we gazed out at the rolling ocean.

"We have to move forward, don't we?"

"That is correct."

"It's just..." I sighed. "The ways of evil cut so deep. It *hurts* to keep going."

"I agree. But you are never alone, Cair. The Voice is always present. And there are angels who love you. Securitie. Myself. I meant what I said earlier. Even though Hurrikiller is dead, you need to forgive him. Let the Voice heal your heart."

Gard held up four fingers. "Many years ago, four angels visited this island. But during their next visit, there were..." he put down one finger. "Only three. And now..." Gard put down another finger. "There are only two. *Please,* Cair."

The pain in his eyes was real.

"I do not wish to be alone on my next visit here."

MIND OVER MATTER

Gard returned to Licemah to inventory the weapons recovered from the ruins, so I decided to visit Lily. The moonlight guided me to the yellow bubble of enérgeia swirling west of the river. My wings pushed me through the barrier and into the sanctuary of the Garden.

Night never fell in this place. Giant butterflies perched on the ten-foot-tall flowers. Frogs and fish swam in the pond. And the smells! So clean, so peaceful. They eased the pain in my troubled mind.

I landed by the willow tree at the water's edge. A familiar water lily bobbed on the blue surface close by. The white petals waved at me. I heard a voice in my head that was full of love and life.

Cair! So good to see you!

The voice once belonged to a green-eyed angel with shoulder-length auburn hair.

Hey, Lily, I replied. *How are you?*

Better, now that I see you. Gard told me you survived the battle when he was here earlier.

He saw you? He still has your petals.

There was a brief pause. *Does he? Well, I'm sure he was just too distracted to tell me.*

I heard the awkwardness in her voice. Years ago, Lily felt attraction love to Gard. But he never realized it until it was too late. Not that it mattered. The Voice lets us feel *all* kinds of love, so we can empathize and minister to His other creations.

The image of Protex smearing the black Hate fruit across my face came to mind and I started crying. Through my shaking sobs, I told Lily what he was doing to me. She listened until my voice trailed away into silence.

Cair, I'm so sorry this is happening to you!

I rubbed my eyes. *I thought since Hurrikiller died, I'd be free of those visions. But now, Protex is using them to...to...*

...to hurt you. Lily finished.

It does hurt, Lily. Like a thorn digging into my skin.

Tell Gard. Or Foster. I'm sure they would help you like they did before.

A giant butterfly hummed as it glided above us on the way to its next flower.

Thanks, Lily. I'm glad you're still here.

I meandered along the path towards the barrier. The creek gurgled as it wound through the Garden. I counted six regular-sized flowers along the banks. These were slain angels waiting for the Voice to give them new bodies. I often thought about the choice I'd make if I was killed. Would I become a flower to wait for a new body? Or would I go to God's Country for everlasting rest?

"Good evening!"

The sudden words were so loud that my hand filled with enérgeia. An angel came walking up the path, waving at me. When I saw who he was, I made the enérgeia disappear.

"Foster!" I exclaimed. "It's not evening, you know!"

"Sure it is," the grinning angel said as he stopped next to me. "This whole bubble is an illusion. If I wanted to say 'Good morning!', then it would be morning. 'Good mornings' are only reserved for mornings."

The teacher angel tapped his beaky nose.

"Okay, Cair, a little enérgeia lesson for you. As angels, we can manipulate objects with yellow light called enérgeia, right? We can shape this light into solid, liquid or gas. Hey! Did you just yawn?"

I closed my mouth. "Sorry, Foster. It's been a long day."

He stared at me with piercing brown eyes. "I get that, but just stay with me."

A ball of enérgeia appeared in his palm. "Enérgeia always leaves signs of where it has been. Tell me, where would you see signs of past enérgeia?"

I tried to think. "Um, like on bodies? Where angels have healed each other?"

The ball vanished when Foster snapped his fingers. "Yes! Anywhere else?"

He looked at me expectantly. I shook my head.

"I'll give you a hint."

Foster pointed at his bald head.

"Your head?"

Foster sighed. "What's *inside* your head, Cair? *Your mind.*"

Now he had my attention.

"After the battle," Foster continued. "I could sense a certain *dark* enérgeia in your mind. Think of it as a parasite."

"Thanks. That makes me feel *so* much better."

He bobbed his head up and down. "You're welcome. Protex is in your *mind.* He is engaging you in some kind of psychological warfare. This is unprecedented! We know enérgeia can affect matter, like solid, liquid and gas. But the mind does not fall into any of those categories! If we can know how he got *in* your mind…"

"…then we can know how to get him *out*," I finished.

Foster pumped his fist in the air. "Time for me to get to work, then! Oh, and on a completely unrelated matter, I put together Tracking enérgeia for Gentull. However, some demon's enérgeia keeps me from locking on to his location. As soon as I break through, you'll be the first to know."

Suddenly, we lost our balance and stumbled to our knees. I closed my eyes and immediately felt connected to the Link. A powerful, loving presence pulled me into His embrace.

Cair, the Voice rumbled. *Welcome, little one. You hear Me as only speaking to you, yet My words go forth to all your brothers and sisters. I am aware of your pain. Protex seeks to destroy you, for he knows your great worth.*

It hurts me, God. Will You take it away?

Something wet dripped on my head. It brought coolness as it sank into my scalp.

I have given you compassion. It will not stop your visions, but it will help you understand why you have them. If Protex succeeds, the cost will be many innocent lives. But fear not. I will be your strength when you are weak. As a father lion looks after his cubs, so shall I look out for you.

I felt the compassion swirl through my head, numbing the dark enérgeia within it.

Tomorrow will be a new day, the Voice continued. *The battle with the demons has turned your home into rubble. Do not worry, for I now give you the entire world of Blueshade as your new home. Make dwellings where you will. Tomorrow is the day Creation will be restored!*

Yellow lights crisscrossed over my body and they filled me with anticipation.

Since evil has robbed Me of one race, I shall create another. And I will set My angels as helpers to it. You will teach these beings My ways. You will show them the ways of peace. And they will glorify Me through their mighty deeds.

The Voice paused and I felt His joy.

My angels, come to the Garden at sunrise. There, we will begin.

THE WEDDING

The morning sun chased the night shadows away from the land. We gathered around the swirling ball of light which quickly changed into the form of an angel.

"Let the entire world be witness to this day," the Voice rumbled. He landed on top of the dome. The enérgeia swirled faster and faster until it was absorbed by Him. He flew down and we followed.

We landed north of the pond near a grove of trees. Apples, oranges and other fruit hung from the branches. Every flower turned toward Him and basked in His light. The butterflies and birds were joined by other animals. Trills and squawks mingled with hoots and snorts. All of Creation seemed to be holding its breath, waiting.

The white light swirled across the Voice's body as He knelt down beside the muddy bank. He grabbed His chest and pulled away a piece of light with His right hand. With His left, He scooped up a clod of dirt from the ground. He folded both hands together and fused the two materials. The dirt hardened into a solid like a rock. It started to grow bigger. Next, the Voice broke the growing rock into two pieces. He laid these pieces on the ground. They grew six feet long as they took distinct forms.

The new beings resembled wingless angels. Both were as brown as the dirt they had come from. The being on the left was male. The one on the right was female.

The Voice knelt down between them and placed a hand over each being. With tingling excitement, I remembered the day I was created and given my name.

"Awake."

Both beings inhaled, and their eyes opened. A deep brown color flecked with gold. Their bodies jerked as they looked up at the Voice's swirling body.

"Do not fear," He told them as He helped them to their feet. "You are My children, whom I love. Look upon the home I now give you."

Their curious eyes took in their surroundings. They pointed at the animals. A buffalo twitched its ears while dogs wagged their tails. I felt the Voice radiating with approval. He turned to the male.

"Your name is Man. You will take care of this world and honor My name in both word and deed. You will be the father of all humans."

The being called Man gave a big, toothy grin. He touched his fingers to his forehead and nodded. The Voice slapped him on the back playfully and Man laughed.

The Voice turned to the female. "Your name is Woman. You will take care of this world and raise your offspring to walk in the ways I will teach you. You will be the mother of all humans."

She bowed low, her curtain of curly black hair swaying slightly. The Voice put His hand to her cheek and she closed her eyes at His touch. Then, He nudged her toward Man. She looked him up and down. Man's mouth hung open. But quickly, he closed it and held out his hand. Smiling, Woman took it and moved her body next to his.

The Voice was now walking between the trees. "Man and Woman, I give you the fruit in these trees as your food. They will satisfy your hunger. Do not eat the meat of the animals; if you do, I will not be able to save you. You will lose many good things that I give you."

The beings' smiles faltered. But then the Voice stripped a branch of two apples and handed them to His new creations. They took them and bit into the fruit carefully. Suddenly, their expressions changed to delight and they took bigger bites. When only the seeds remained, the Voice took them and buried them in the ground.

"New trees will grow where you plant them," He said. "In this manner, you and your offspring will always have plenty. For the world of Blueshade stretches beyond the Garden."

Suddenly, we all were floating high in the atmosphere. The two humans chattered excitedly as they pointed down at the three continents below. They had no idea what had went on the last hundred years. They didn't understand what the patches of black represented.

My world, you are made as new.

The world responded to the Voice's thunderous command. A wave of green spread across the black areas of the Mainland, the Peninsula and the Tip. The humans watched with wide eyes and growing smiles. I felt Creation sighing as its scars were healed. I imagined the demons racing for shelter below as the Voice restored the land.

Time sped up as we fell back to earth. Man and Woman drew closer together, holding hands, watching as the sun was replaced by the moon and the stars. Night had fallen across the Garden, the first night it had ever seen. The giant tulips had already closed their petals and fireflies weaved through the air. The humans kept looking up at the stars twinkling in the black sky. I realized it was the first night they'd ever seen, too.

Our feet touched down in the open clearing. A gleaming white altar had appeared by the creek. The edges curled in spirals of marble. We angels spread out in a semicircle around the two humans. Gard helped Man into a white robe. Incurajuh helped Woman into another one. The robes wrapped around their naked bodies.

The Voice stood before the altar. He raised His hands and white light spun in tight circles around them. The white changed to different colors: red, blue, green and black. Each new color split from the circle and hardened into sparkling jewels. Ruby, sapphire, emerald, diamond. The remaining white light hardened into a pearl. There was another flash of light, and then each jewel was set in a golden ring.

The five rings floated into the Voice's hand.

"Today, we are gathered to witness the union between Man and Woman," He declared with pride in each word. "For the marriage between these two is a sacred covenant. It embodies the four kinds of love."

He gestured for the two humans to approach Him. They did.

"Friendship love, the love that includes, enjoys and celebrates community."

The Voice handed the five rings to Man.

"Attraction love, the love that chooses, celebrates intimacy and leads to offspring."

Woman held out a trembling hand as Man put each ring on one of her fingers.

"Family love, the love that nurtures offspring, gives grace and celebrates kinship."

Man and Woman, side by side, fingers intertwined, faced the Voice.

"And, finally, the greatest love of all. Unconditional love, the love that moves mountains, parts rivers and mirrors the love I have for you. Man and Woman. Do you both swear to love each other with these four kinds of love?"

"We do," they answered.

The Voice bowed His head. "Then I proclaim you husband and wife. Be good to each other. You may seal this marriage with a kiss."

And they did. Man and Woman shared a long kiss, eyes closed, enjoying the moment. Securitie whooped with joy and started clapping her hands together. The rest of us joined in with applause. Bellows, shrieks and howls from the animals showed their approval. Man and Woman broke apart, their faces red. They ran to the Voice, Who gathered them under His arms. Tears of happiness flowed from their eyes as they gazed up at Him.

Like children to their father, I thought and remembered the monument in Licemah.

The Voice escorted the humans out of the clearing in an embrace that no demon could break.

THE LOST CENTURY

And so was the beginning of the time-bending part in history we angels called the Lost Century. One-hundred years passed in one-hundred days. The Voice compressed the flow of time; each day was actually an entire year. It showed the awesome power of the Voice and enabled the humans to grow in number.

Through attraction love, Woman gave birth to twenty-four children. Each baby had a different skin color. Some were brown like their parents. Others were olive or tan or pale like the moon. But Man and Woman loved them all the same. The family lived under an enormous thatch roof held up by thatch walls. When each baby was born, an angel would present them with a white robe. This robe was enchanted with enérgeia and stretched as the infant grew.

About the thirtieth year, several brothers married their sisters and moved into thatch dwellings of their own. By the sixtieth year, mankind had spread across the Mainland. The next generation had begun, as Man and Woman's children started having children themselves.

Dozens of thatch roundhouses were built along the banks of the Frost River; inside the forests of the east; deep in the valleys between the Glacier Mountains; all lands between the eastern desert and the western savannah were now populated by these new beings.

Each angel helped the humans in some special way. Foster taught them how to tell the time of day based on where the sun was in the sky. Incurajuh showed them how to help care for animals. Securitie taught them how to make jokes. And Gard introduced them to tools, which helped them build more structures than just thatch roundhouses.

"Are you *sure* they'll be okay on those?" I asked him one day as we watched them carve something new.

"They have progressed from thatch to wood," Gard noted as we watched three men lay rectangular planks on top of longer ones. "Very diligent, these humans. They lack enérgeia, so they must rely on whatever resources they can find."

The new structure eventually became a boat. The men celebrated their accomplishment with their wives and children. They stocked woven baskets with fruit and carried them on to the boat.

"I guess they'll be okay on the ocean, right? They don't have wings like we do."

"Why, Cair," Gard said, chuckling. "It sounds like you are *concerned* for them."

"Blueshade's a *big* world and the humans are *tiny*."

"We know every part of the Blueshade," Gard continued. "Now it is mankind's turn to explore this world."

And explore it they did. Over the next year, many boats crossed the oceans. One family had landed theirs on Volcano Island. They built three huts on the southern beach. In the midday heat, the family would splash in the surf, laughing as the waves knocked them over. The men constructed bonfires at night and the women danced, their shadows stretching across the sand.

I don't know why I stayed there watching them. Maybe it was the simple joy they showed in how they lived each day. But this island held memories of pain and sadness for me. In the clearing under the volcano, Hurr had accidently wounded me with a poisonous toxitrike horn. That incident started Hurr down a path where I couldn't follow him.

One day I decided to visit the human family. The mother Zanesu was one of Man and Woman's children. But it was Zanesu's children who intrigued me the most. Bale was a leader among the older boys who spent their days climbing trees and skipping stones across the jungle streams. His sister Raliga helped her mother weave baskets and make necklaces. Both shared a spirit of quiet joy.

I came to them in the evening. All fourteen were sitting around the bonfire and eating bananas and pineapples. I approached them slowly, because different humans reacted in different ways when they saw us. Some found us intimidating because we were taller, but this family welcomed me. The humans waved enthusiastically and pointed to an open spot in the sand. Right between Bale and Raliga. They invited me to sit down. I did so, criss-crossing my legs under me. I held up my hand politely when they offered me some of their fruit.

"No," I said to them. "I do not eat food. But I do bring a gift."

I unbuckled the satchel from around my waist. In the sand before me, I laid out three items: a scroll, an egret feather and a small bottle of ink. I smoothed out the scroll until it was flat. Then, I dipped the tip of the feather into the ink and wrote a single line across the top of the scroll. I handed the scroll to Bale who stared at it with wide eyes.

"Words," I told him. "You can write the words you speak on this scroll."

His family watched Bale as he copied my mark. I nodded with approval. Then Bale hunched over the scroll and drew a dozen symbols and letters. He pointed to them with one hand and pointed to his face with the other.

"Bale," he said slowly. "My name is Bale. I live on Volcano Island with my family."

Shouts filled the air as his family descended upon him. His mother kissed him, his father squeezed his shoulders and his cousins danced around the bonfire. Raliga kneeled down next to the scroll and began writing on it herself. Her sleek black hair hid what she was doing. The noise died down and the family, too, was watching.

Raliga cleared her throat and lifted the scroll for all to see. Fourteen stick figures stood next to a hump.

"My family!" Raliga shouted with pride. "You are words now, too!"

"What is the hump, sister?" Bale asked.

"The hump is the volcano!"

In the commotion that followed, each family member had a turn with the quill. They eagerly discussed what they might draw or write. When the last little boy put down the quill, the family gazed on the scroll with wonder. The names of each human were scrawled at the top. The middle had scattered letters here and there. The bottom now had rocks, huts, trees, fish and a few drawings that looked like ocean waves. Zanesu raised her hand.

"Family, we have words to *write* and pictures to *draw*."

She faced me and bowed low. "Thank you, angel."

Thirteen people repeated the phrase as they bowed as well. I rose to my full height and unfolded my wings.

"I appreciate your kind words. But do not bow to me. The Voice has given you this gift. I am but a messenger. May these things bring you more laughs, more smiles and more understanding of how much He loves you. Praise His Name!"

"Praise His Name!"

But as those words of adoration floated from my mouth, I suddenly felt troubled in my mind. It was like some dark presence lurked behind my eyes and looked out at the dancing humans like they were food.

THE FIRST REALM

The introduction of written language was a great gift for mankind. Bale learned how to make new scrolls from the papyrus plant. He obtained papyrus from the jungle and planted several crops near the huts. With the moist soil and open sunlight, the papyrus plants grew ten feet tall. He then sliced the stalks into smaller pieces and laid them in water to soak for a day. Next, he'd beat them hard with his fist, then easy with a smooth stone. Finally, he'd have a scroll to write on.

News of this incredible process spread across the world. Other humans came to Volcano Island to learn from him. Bale wrote down real stories and made-up ones. Real stories of treks into the jungle to gather fruit. Made-up stories involving flying dolphins and birds that could swim underwater. He wrote nearly one-hundred tales.

As Bale duplicated the scroll, his sister duplicated the ink and quill. Raliga would comb the island and the beaches for bird feathers. She soon had quite a collection. The feathers came from red macaws, blue parrots, green parakeets, pink flamingos, white pelicans and black cormorants. Raliga also experimented with volcano soot, honey and water to create ink. The ink was stored in uprooted tree trunks that had been hollowed out. She even learned how to mix dye from different plants to create colored ink.

Raliga quickly became the island's best picture-drawer. She sketched plants, animals, seashells and many other things. Her creativity impressed everyone around her, including a boy her age. She eventually married him. Bale married a girl who was also a storyteller. Both of Zanesu's children soon had children of their own.

Within the last year of the Lost Century, the three huts became a village of twelve. The islanders built little boats they called canoes, which they steered with paddles. They used these to explore the rest of the island. The humans on Volcano Island were developing their own rituals, their own routines and their own way of life.

The Lost Century ended, but time marched on. Mankind had spread across the three continents, but none had formed a society like Bale's people. Even the other angels felt the impact of this significant milestone. In mid-Summer of the year 602, all of them flew to the island. Today was going to be a special day. It would be the day the humans would form the first *realm*.

Men, women and children all gathered by the firepit in two lines. The other angels and I stood in the lines, too. Bale approached the firepit from the east. At the same time, his son Bacaniber approached from the west. They met in the middle. Bacaniber crouched while Bale remained standing.

"My family," Bale called out above the surf. "For many years, this island has been our home. The Voice has truly blessed us. Now is the time we say our name to the world. I put forth my son, Bacaniber as our people's chieftain. Will you accept him?"

"We will accept him," the others echoed.

Bale nodded and lowered himself to a crouch. At the same time, Bacaniber stood up. He had his father's brown eyes and nimble fingers.

"My family," Bacaniber addressed them. "I am honored. By the Voice's will, *our* people will now be known as the Bacaniber people. When our island is drawn on maps, the name will stand out in bold letters. We are *Bacaniber Island!*"

From under his robe, he pulled out a long scroll. His father rose and helped him unroll it to its full length. On it, a picture of a blue dolphin jumping over a star in a green sky.

"Let us hang this flag proudly above the doorways of our homes," Bacaniber continued. "Let our kin across the world know us as the Bacaniber Tribe! Praise the Voice!"

The islanders cheered and broke formation, hugging each other and their new chieftain.

12

GUARDIAN ANGEL

"These humans like to dance," Incurajuh observed.

The two of us sat in the wet sand. Waves surged up around us before being pulled back out to sea. Remnants of the midday meal included banana peels and coconut husks. A trio of men pounded a beat on coconut husks while a dozen women danced in a circle. Bale and Bacaniber played a throwing game with rocks while Raliga braided her niece's hair.

"They're very happy," I agreed. "How are the other humans doing?"

Incurajuh smiled. "They eat, they laugh, they play. Every animal gets along with them. They manage resources well. If they pick all the fruit from a tree, they plant the seeds so new trees can grow."

Our conversation was interrupted by a ball of white light that fell from the sky. It landed next to Bacaniber and took the form of an angel.

"Bacaniber, son of Bale," the Voice said.

All the humans fell to their knees. All angels bowed their heads.

"Mighty Voice," Bacaniber spoke to the ground. "Here I am."

"You have declared your family as the Bacaniber Tribe?"

"Yes."

"Then it is so," the Voice rumbled with approval. "Your realm of Bacaniber Island is the first realm of man. Each realm will need a guardian." He turned His face towards us. "Which one of you will be Bacaniber Island's Guardian Angel? Before you answer, know this: the angel who leads this realm of men can no longer come and go as he or she pleases. They will be bound to this realm forever, or until death."

Bound to this realm? I thought. *If that angel stayed here forever, he or she wouldn't see the rest of Blueshade.*

"I will," Incurajuh called out from beside me. "I will become Bacaniber Island's Guardian Angel."

The wind gusted around her and swirled her dark hair across her face.

"It is done," the Voice declared. "Rise, and continue your celebration!"

The Voice disappeared. The Bacanibers stood again and gazed at Incurajuh. Then, they broke into smiles and ran towards her. I stepped out of the way, laughing as she was embraced by the community. The display of their affection caught her off guard.

"Oh!" Incurajuh said in surprise. "Thank you...hello...nice to meet you, too..."

A young girl pressed a bracelet of tiny blue-and-yellow shells into her hands.

"Abalones from the reef," the girl said and pointed at the ocean. "Papa brings them back sometimes. It's yours, angel. Put it on!"

Incurajuh slipped the bracelet on her wrist. Immediately, the shells changed colors to red-and-green. She smiled at the girl.

"These are beautiful iridescent shells! Thank you for your gift, young one."

I kept laughing as the community pulled her toward the firepit.

"These people will be good for her."

Gard sidled up next to me. We watched as Bale shared a scroll with Incurajuh.

"Hey, Gard, would you be a Guardian Angel if another realm came to be?"

"I do not have an answer, Cair. To serve these new beings would be a great respite from the horrors of war we have endured."

Before I could respond, Foster trundled over with an excited look on his face. Another angel with windswept blonde hair followed him. He clenched a scroll in his hand. It was Kumpashin, who I'd accidentally knocked over in Licemah.

"It is happening!" Foster exclaimed. "The Tracking enérgeia is breaking through!"

Gard put a restraining hand on his shoulder. "Let us relocate our discussion."

We left the Bacaniber village behind and flew up to the rim of the volcano. Lava bubbled deep in the crater below. Gard nodded with satisfaction.

"Good, the magma remains where it should. Now, Foster, tell us again what..."

"The demons," Foster interrupted and cracked his knuckles. "Those bat-wings always underestimate the persistence of Tracking enérgeia. Kumpashin, show them your map."

The other angel unrolled his scroll. I saw a picture of the Peninsula, the continent far to the east. A red circle was drawn around an area on the western coast.

"You see the heavy woods across the north?" Kumpashin asked. "But on the coast *here* are the Honeycomb Cliffs. *That's* where they're keeping Gentull."

Gard sighed. "Queen Bee's hive runs under those cliffs."

"The enérgeia shows he's in the deepest tunnel," Kumpashin rolled up the scroll. "The hive is, like, *huge*. It'd be like finding a fish in the ocean."

"Or a needle in a haystack," Foster offered. "I *assume* you know what a needle is? The little tool humans use to fix tears in their robes?"

"So, it should take us a month to fly there if we left right now?" I asked Gard.

The teacher angel looked at Foster. "I remember you said you were working on an enérgeia similar to the demons' way of teleportation. Have you completed it?"

"Yeah, I'm full of surprises," Foster answered. "The Teleportation enérgeia can get you there in less than a minute. But it's only a one-way trip. *This* enérgeia is still in the works."

A flock of brightly-colored parrots soared across the jungle treetops below. I imagined the hive, closed-in, dark and stuffy. Then I remembered Gentull bellowing defiantly at the ring of Shadows tightening around him.

My hands balled into fists. "How do we get back?"

"Praise the Voice for Lily," Gard said and pulled his hand from his robe. Three white flower petals lay in his palm. "Petals from the flower of a transformed angel have special properties. While inside our mouth, they will transport us back here."

He gave me one of the petals, which I tucked inside my sleeve. Suddenly, Gard gasped and fell to his knees. Before I could bend down to help, he stood up straight and unfurled his wings.

"Cair, the Voice has called me for something urgent," Gard said in a troubled tone. "You must go to Gentull now! I am sorry I cannot accompany you. Another angel will need to go in my place."

Kumpashin stepped forward. "I'll go."

Gard gave him the two other petals. "One for you, one for Gentull."

"Gard," I said. "What's going on?"

He met my gaze with alert eyes.

"Please, Cair, there is no time to waste! Foster, send them now!"

Foster shrugged and his hands blazed with enérgeia.

"Don't forget to eat your flowers!"

IN THE HIVE
OF THE QUEEN

The roaring surf thundered in my ears. The gray-green waves broke upon the jagged rocks that littered the beach. Kumpashin was next to me. He squinted at something above us.

"You don't see that every day."

I followed his gaze. Massive two-hundred-foot cliffs towered over us. Seven or eight large holes marked the white chalk surface like spots on a leopard. I wondered where all the bees were. There must be more openings at the top.

"Ready?" I asked Kumpashin.

He puffed his hair out of his eyes but the wind fluttered it back. He sighed and unrolled a golden whip from his belt. "How many bees you think live in there?"

"Hurrikiller once said the queen had four battalions at one time. But I don't think there's that many now. Some died during the war. There might be five or six-hundred left."

Kumpashin swallowed hard. "Five or six-hundred. Right."

I looked at him curiously. "Kumpashin, are you okay?"

"Yeah. Bees just have those creepy eyes, you know? They don't blink."

"I'll understand if you can't..."

He shook his head. "I'd rather fight a dragon than, like, something with six legs. But I'm good."

We glided up the cliffside until we came to the first six-sided hole.

"The opening's a hexagon." Kumpashin observed. "Probably more hexagons inside."

I gazed past him into the tunnel. "What are you talking about?"

"Oh, I like numbers and shapes," he continued. "It helps when I have a problem with giant insects. With hexagons all over the place, it means the hive is sturdy and grounded."

As we crept down the tunnel, I could see Kumpashin was right. A deep thrumming sound increased with each step we took. The walls were covered in six-sided honeycombs. Honey dripped from them and made the floor warm and sticky. A sickly smell made me wrinkle my nose.

"Honey is supposed to smell sweet," I whispered.

"Yeah," Kumpashin agreed. "I wonder if it's too much honey in one place?"

He suddenly yelled and raised his whip high.

A dead bee lay tangled in the honey in front of us. The insect was the size of a cow. Black stripes zigzagged across its fuzzy yellow body and the lifeless compound eyes stared into space. Kumpashin shivered and lowered his whip.

"That's really gross."

I focused my eyes on the honeycomb wall. "How much farther to Gentull?"

"Just a little bit."

We encountered three more dead bees as we went deeper into the hive. We had to change tunnels twice to avoid the living ones. I tried not to think about how long we'd been in here.

"So, Kumpashin, did you get those weapons to Gard?"

"Uh, what weapons?"

I stopped walking. "The weapons you had when I knocked you over, remember?"

"You didn't knock me...hang on a second..."

Kumpashin knelt down. He ran his hand over a dry spot.

"I don't get it. Gentull should be, like, *right here.*"

Suddenly, the floor cracked beneath us and we fell through the hole. The deep thrumming sound became louder and faster. Blurs of yellow and black darted around me. Before my wings could open, I landed in a pool of honey. It covered my body in its stickiness. My arms and legs moved ridiculously slow. I couldn't even raise them from the liquid!

The hole we'd fallen through was five-hundred feet above me. The underground cavern could've swallowed the Voice's Temple in Licemah. Stalactites grew from the ceiling, while stalagmites rose from the floor like teeth. Dozens of holes looked like they'd been smashed into the floor. All were empty except for one; beneath a protective layer of some gooey material, the shadow of something tiny squirmed around.

Giant bees buzzed furiously overhead. We were lucky not to have landed on them; their stingers were five inches thick. Each would land on the cavern wall and after clicking their mandibles together, they would resume their agitated flight.

"Cair? Are you stuck in honey, too?"

Kumpashin's voice called out from somewhere to my right. I tried moving my arm.

"Hang on, I'm trying to get free!"

You have no freedom while I command it.

The bees scattered as their queen loomed from the shadows. She was the size of an elephant. Her gigantic wings held her bloated body in the air. Each fuzzy hair bristled like a spear. Her eyes stared at us unblinking.

I tried to concentrate on my enérgeia. Maybe the honey could change to water. Then I'd be free. But the queen's haughty voice continued.

She was right about the invaders. Once she has you, she will restore our colony.

"Small colonies can be nice, you know!" Kumpashin called out.

Queen Bee flicked her antenna. *You ignorant two-leg! Have you not seen the bodies as you came down the tunnels? These are all the drones of my colony who remain!*

The other bees now hovered around her, buzzing softly.

Since the demon leader has died, my honey grows sour. My drones die easier. My babies do not hatch. Only one remains.

"Is *this* the one you mean?"

The queen turned her vast bulk around; the enormous wings sat her on the ground before folding. The cavern shook as from her gigantic footfalls. The other bees buzzed in alarm and flew out of my line of sight. I had to see what was going on!

With a squelching noise, I yanked my upper body from the honey. To my right, I saw Kumpashin, with only one leg still stuck. He caught my gaze and put a finger to his lips. He made a turning motion with his hands and I looked to my left.

Two demons were tearing into the gooey material with their claws. The taller one snarled and tossed the gooey material to the floor. The shorter one reached in and pulled out something that looked like a sickly, pale, squirming worm with legs.

"Leverage, says I! Just what we need!"

Queen Bee's voice shook the cavern. Some of the honeycombs dropped from above.

WHAT IS THE MEANING OF THIS? ARE YOU HERS?

"No, we ain't hers," the shorter demon growled.

YOU WILL NOT HAVE MY BABY!!!

The other bees aimed their stingers at the two demons and slowly closed in on them.

"None of that!" The taller one shook his fist. "Unless you want the queen's last baby to be *terminated.*"

Stop! Do not move closer, Queen Bee ordered. The drones landed beside her. Their antennae moved back and forth. One drone tilted his head towards the queen as if waiting for new orders. The taller demon chuckled and he elbowed his companion.

"I said *terminated*. Get it? Because they're insects."

Great, I thought to myself. *It's Kunsern and Kunsiderut from the swamp. Of course.*

Kumpashin and I pulled the rest of our bodies from the honey. I limped over to him. He tried getting the honey out of his hair, but gave up trying. I still had clumps in mine. We crept along the wall and stayed in the shadows.

"Hand over your prisoner," Kunsiderut demanded. "And we'll release your filthy brat, says I."

The pupa squirmed in his hands. Some gooey green liquid oozed from its body.

"Show me 'im, now!" Kunsiderut snarled and shook the pupa harder.

The queen dropped her head in defeat. *Fetch the prisoner.*

Two of the drones disappeared up one of the tunnels. The gooey green liquid now dripped from Kunsiderut's arms. He shuddered and looked around at the cavern walls.

"Yucky place, says I. Why'd she bring 'im here?"

Kunsern shrugged. "Don't know. Ah, here he comes now!"

The two bees flew back from the tunnel and dropped an angel at the demons' feet. I stifled a sob. It was Gentull; but not the Gentull I knew. His trembling arms and legs were curled tight against his body. His white robe had been replaced by an ugly brown one that had holes in it. He gazed blankly into space, like he was detached from the events around him.

Kunsiderut kicked him hard in the back. Then, the demon tossed the squirming pupa up high.

14

ALLEGIANCE

Queen Bee trumpeted like an elephant and reared up on her legs, trying to reach her pupa. But the pupa continued soaring higher. The drones shot after it; before the pupa could smash against the ceiling, one of them caught it with his legs.

Kumpashin's whip flicked past me and popped Kunisderut on his foot. The demon yowled and hopped around while clutching his toes. I sent blasts of enérgeia from each hand at him. But he hopped out of the way and the blasts smashed through the wall. The cavern shook again.

My subjects! The queen shrieked. *I want no more part in a demon war! We will build a new hive. Begone!*

Using her girth, Queen Bee slammed through the ceiling. The drones followed her, including the one that clutched her pupa. Stalactites dropped and shattered on the floor. I dodged a bolt of dark enérgeia that shot from Kunsern's hands. His next would've caught me if he hadn't tripped over a stalagmite. He landed in a pool of honey and I left him floundering in it.

Kumpashin was kneeling over Gentull's twitching body. He forced a white petal into Gentull's mouth. Gentull vanished from the spot. Kumpashin sighed with relief as he stood.

"Get down!" I yelled and threw a yellow ball that just missed him. It splattered against Kunsiderut who'd been creeping up behind him.

"Not more gooey stuff!"

The demon snarled and tried to wipe the yellow sludge from his robe. He spat on the floor and glared at me. Black enérgeia swirled between his fingers.

"Ain't got no giant bird to save you *this* time, says I! You...are..."

His face slackened and the black enérgeia fizzled out. He gazed at the ceiling. Even Kumpashin and Kunsern had frozen in place to see what was happening. When I looked up, I saw why.

A demon floated down through the hole Queen Bee had left behind. Diamonds adorned the collar of her black robe. Raven hair trailed like a banner behind her. She landed on a large rock and retracted her leathery wings. All of Queen Bee's references to 'she' and 'hers' made since now. The last time I saw this demon was in the middle of a forest fire.

"Kunsern and Kunsiderut," Sage hissed. "Of course, it'd be *you two*."

Kunsiderut's face slowly turned red. Kunsern pulled his left arm from the honey. Sage tilted her head to the side as she observed Kumpashin.

"Huh? I thought Gard would come himself. But instead, there's Kumpashin and…"

Her yellow eyes locked on me.

"Cair? Gard sent *you*? A pity. I would've like to hear his last words before I killed him."

She looked around the cavern. "Where's my prisoner? You didn't help him escape, did you?"

"He's gone, Sage," I said, bringing myself to look at her. "You won't hurt him anymore."

Sage stroked her diamonds. "At least *you* got him, Cair, instead of the *buffoons* Protex sent."

"Shut your mouth, says I!" Kunsiderut spat. His face was fully red now. He glanced at Kunsern, who was finally free from the honey. "Ain't you tired of being bullied all the time?"

Kunsern shrugged. "Yes. But I also like staying alive."

The taller demon knelt down before Sage. "I swear allegiance to you, Sage."

Kunsiderut screamed in rage and lunged at Kunsern. Suddenly, Sage stood between them and caught Kunsiderut by his neck.

"You would attack one of my own?" Sage tutted. "I didn't know you were *that* much of a buffoon."

Kunsiderut made gagging noises and his claws tried to break her grip. Kumpashin crept up next to me. His hand slid into his robe.

"I want you to give Protex a message," Sage continued. "I know about his plan. Tell him I am going to get there first."

She snarled and threw him into the cavern wall. "What are you waiting for? Go, now!"

Kunsiderut wheezed as he picked himself off the floor. He unfurled his wings and flew towards the hole in the ceiling. Sage watched him. When he was almost there, a cruel smile spread over her face.

"I LIED!!!" Sage bellowed.

She swiped her arms in a vertical motion. Kunsiderut plummeted back down and crashed down on top of some sharp stalagmites. I turned my head. Beside me, Kumpashin pushed something soft into my hand. I had barely closed my fist around it when I was blasted off my feet.

"Now, now, none of that! We need to catch up!"

I rolled across the floor. When I stopped, the enérgeia rose from my hands and formed a yellow shield. Just in time for the black bolts to break on it. Pushing my hair from my eyes, I looked around for the little white flower petal. *Where was it?*

"Do you need this?" Sage mocked, holding it between her fingers. "Why? We're having so much...*fun!*"

She swiped her free hand in a horizontal motion. My body was yanked out from behind the shield. I spun in circles until I collided painfully with Sage's rock. Spots danced before my eyes and I stumbled to my feet. Before I could regain my balance, I heard her cackle.

"What was that trick you showed me last time? Oh, yeah, this one!"

This time, my body floated through the air like a feather. I rose to the ceiling. My legs kicked the air uselessly. I hovered right over the stalagmites that killed Kunsiderut, his body directly beneath me.

Sage bared her teeth. "Oh, Cair. Hurrikiller *never* loved you! *I* was his fav..."

A huge honeycomb slammed against her back. Sage moaned as she fell to her knees. I screamed as I plummeted towards the stalagmites. A whoosh of warm air pushed me to the right and I landed on the cavern floor. Kumpashin yanked me to my feet and pressed the petal into my hand once more.

"Go, Cair!" He yelled and stuffed his own into his mouth.

I did the same. The cavern began to spin. I saw Kunsern trapped by the golden whip and Sage rising, her scream filling my ears. Something shiny flew from her hand.

Then, the cavern disappeared.

15

THE TRAP

I blinked in the evening sunset. Green trees. Bird sounds from the jungle. Bacaniber Island.

"Welcome back, Cair," Foster said.

The world was still spinning. I stumbled and he caught me.

"Easy, now. Drink this potion and I swear you'll feel *almost* better."

I drank from the vial. A cool feeling spread over me and the world came back into focus.

"Wh-what do you mean '*almost better*?'" I sputtered.

Foster pointed behind him. "The good news is they made it back."

Two fiber-made sleeping bags lay side by side. Kumpashin lay on his back, with both hands folded on his stomach. His eyes were closed and his breathing shallow.

"He had a knife in there," Foster said. "He'll be fine after some rest."

"What about Gentull?"

Foster rubbed the back of his neck. "He was here. Then Incurajuh took him to some kind of hot spring. She said he'll live."

I sank to my knees. "Praise the Voice, we got him out of there."

Foster joined me. "Indeed. You fared better than I would've. Oh, remember when I said that you'd feel *almost* better? The bad news is that the humans have found the Spotless Flock."

"How?"

He looked at me seriously. "If you get pulled into a vision with Protex again, think of how strong you are. You aren't weak. You aren't powerless. You are one of the Voice's angels and He loves you. Don't forget these words."

I inclined my head. "Thanks for saying that. I don't think of myself that way, so it's uplifting when someone else does. Is Gard waiting for me?"

Foster helped me to my feet. "He's at the Frost River mouth on the Mainland."

I left the lush jungle island behind and hurled over the ocean.

The sun was sinking over the loblolly pines when I made it to the Frost River mouth. The river actually started way up in the mountains and snaked down to the coast. Salt and fresh water swirled together in the three-hundred-foot-wide river mouth. Dark clouds rolled across the sky as they signaled an approaching storm.

I landed on the eastern riverbank. Gard wasn't anywhere in sight. Instead, I saw the golden bodies of six ewe and one ram scattered in the grass. Man and Woman stood still as statues. Each held a long spear; the tips were red with blood.

I hurried over to the golden ram.

"What have you done?" I whispered and stroked the soft wool. Then, I looked at the humans.

"WHAT HAVE YOU DONE?!?!?"

They flinched like I had struck them and the spears dropped from their hands. Man averted his eyes while Woman covered her mouth with her hand. She trembled as she held my gaze. Her terrified brown eyes had a shade of green in them.

Suddenly, there was a terrible pain in the back of my leg! The sharpness shot through the rest of my body and dropped me to the ground. I screamed in agony and clutched my leg. My heart pounded faster and I watched a sickly green color slither up across my thigh. Black started ringing my vision. Then I saw the red-haired demon standing over me, holding the purple toxitrike horn.

"Does it *hurt?*" Protex sneered. "Like someone has ripped your heart from your chest?"

I couldn't even get words from my mouth. My body trembled as the poison spread.

"Been working on them for months now," Protex waved the horn at the humans. "Easy to manipulate if you know how."

Thunder boomed overhead and a lightning flash lit up the night.

Then there was nothing.

16

BETTER

The storm had passed and clouds rolled across the night sky, just as a heavy wind rolled across the savannah and bent the tall grass. Thirty-three demons growled as they tried to untangle themselves from one another.

"You're crushing me, says I!" Kunsiderut moaned.

Deefins kicked him away from the pile. "Hard to see you when you're so short!"

With much growling and grumbling, the individual demons crawled out from the mass of bodies. The tall grass parted and a curious rhinoceros lumbered forward. It made a snuffling noise and flared its nostrils. Kunsern clutched his snout.

"Smelly beast. Go away!"

The animal just stood there swishing its tail.

Kunsiderut climbed to his feet and dusted off his black robe. "Eh, what's that? You're a smelly beast yourself! Just look at you, says I!"

Kunsern examined the bumpy skin on his arms.

At the other end of the clearing, Kynd wailed and buried her face in Protex's chest.

"Don't look at me, Protex! I'm hideous!"

Protex gently took her tear-stained face in his claws. "My sweet, you'll always be beautiful to me."

The rhino snorted and took a few tentative steps forward.

"Get lost, you stupid animal!"

Sage screamed in the night. Dark enérgeia shot from her hands in the form of black flames. It incinerated the animal and left behind a pile of ash. The other demons looked at Sage in amazement. She shrugged.

"*What?* Death is in our world now. We might as well get used to it."

A burly demon with a spiked back stalked up to where Hurr was sitting. The burly demon snorted and his breath ruffled Hurr's blonde hair.

"Yeah, and it's *your* fault!"

Hurr kept his eyes on the savannah. "You have a complaint against me, Tenderr?"

"Complaint? Of course, I have a complaint!" Tenderr bellowed and every demon fell silent. "You talk about us taking control. Now, we're *here*, cut off from our angel brethren and cursed by the Voice!"

Hurr sighed. He stood and looked the bigger demon in the eyes. "Actually, you should blame *yourself* for following *me*. *I* am not in charge of *your* actions."

Tenderr roared and lunged forward. With sudden swiftness, Hurr dodged under the muscular arms. Tenderr turned back around, only to find Hurr's snake-hilted sword buried in his large stomach.

Hurr wrenched his sword free. The big demon fell to the ground, lifeless.

"My *brethren*," Hurr addressed the remaining demons as he wiped off his sword. "For I can truly call you that. You have chosen me over the Voice. I don't forget the consequences you now bear *because* of that choice."

He sheathed the sword. "I killed Zafe who tried to keep me from the Spotless Flock. I killed Tenderr who tried to keep me from my new purpose. With a new *purpose* comes a new *name*. From this moment forward, you will address me as Lord Hurrikiller."

Sage was first to bow before him. "Long live Lord Hurrikiller!"

Protex and Kynd bowed next. "Long live Lord Hurrikiller!"

The rest of the demons kneeled down, taking up the cry and Hurrikiller gnashed his teeth together.

"As such, I will lead us in war against the Voice and our once-brothers and once-sisters. From the materials stolen from the forge, we will build our own cities. Cities where we can do whatever we want. And death waits for any *angel* who gets in our way!"

The demons roared with approval.

"Hurr!" I suddenly called out to him. "Hurr! Don't do this!"

He stopped pacing and gazed over the bobbing heads of his followers. Like he was trying to pick out my voice from the dozens of others. Protex turned around. The corners of his mouth twitched.

"Like the past, do you, Cair? Come see what else I've been up to."

The vision changed.

I was in the Garden. Man and Woman were strolling through the flowers, holding hands and laughing. They entered the shady grove and plucked fruit to eat. I tried calling out to them, but to my horror, my body was bound to one of the apple trees. I moved my mouth, but the words wouldn't come.

"'S better if you just watch," Protex whispered. He stepped in front of me, so I could see the horns shrink and feathers grow on his scaly wings.

Protex looked like an angel again.

"Greetings, Man and Woman," he said and walked forward. The humans waved at him.

"Hello, angel of the Voice," Man answered. "How are you today?"

"I'm well."

Protex extended his open hands.

"Today, I bring you a gift," he said as the humans swallowed the last of the fruit. "Please, take my hands."

Woman glanced at Man as if asking for reassurance. Man nodded and grabbed Protex's left hand. Woman grabbed his right. Twin glimmers of green, nearly lost to the morning sunlight, vanished into their fingers. An uneasy feeling swept over me as Protex let go of their hands.

"How does the fruit taste today?"

Man reached up for another apple. "The same as it did yesterday."

"Oh. It *hasn't* grown better in taste?"

He let the words hang. Man's arm stopped mid-reach.

"What do you mean by *better*, angel?"

"Just that there are other kinds of food that taste *better* than these fruits."

Woman bit her lip. "But the Voice has given us *these* fruits to satisfy our hunger."

"Hunger, yes," Protex purred. "But what of taste? The Voice would *want* you to enjoy the tastes of different food."

Woman thought it over. "Yes. What you say is true."

"Where is this new food you speak of?" Man asked.

Protex pointed southeast. "Where the Frost River runs into the ocean."

"Is it *better* fruit than these?" Man asked again.

"It isn't fruit at all. It's animal meat."

Man frowned.

"But it is forbidden!" Woman shouted in disbelief. "The Voice has forbidden us to eat the meat of animals! He said He cannot save us!"

"Save you from what?" Protex laughed and put a hand on her shoulder. It appeared to be a re-assuring gesture. "What kind of a father forbids his children from having better things? The Voice *told* you to take care of His world, yes? What better way than to explore every possibility?"

The golden flecks in her eyes changed to green and her shoulders relaxed.

"What are you doing, angel?" Man asked.

But Protex already had his other hand on his shoulder. Man's flecks also changed to that green color. A satisfied smirk crossed Protex's face as he bent low to whisper in Man's ears.

"The sheep that live by the river mouth are different from any other. Their fleeces are pure gold. Their blood contains power, power that the Voice may not want you to have."

He removed his hands. The two humans stumbled like they had been awakened from a deep sleep.

"Why can't we have this power?" Woman muttered.

"Why does the Voice keep it from us?" Man agreed and put his arm around her.

Protex nodded. "Why, indeed? Travel to this place. Tell none of your children where you are going. I'll meet you there in the trees with weapons. Then, you'll kill the Spotless Flock and discover the secret of their blood."

I struggled against the invisible binds that trapped me. The humans' willpower was crumbling and they would unleash pain and sorrow on a world just healed from war. They started walking toward the creek, speaking softly about their new plan.

"Shame, isn't it?" Protex mocked as he transformed back into his demon self. "To think they could've been protected by you, when you can't even protect yourself."

Foster's words resurfaced in my mind and I focused all my willpower on them.

"I'm not weak!"

The words burst from my mouth, causing Protex to frown.

"I'm not powerless!" I yelled again.

Protex snarled and raised his claws to strike me.

"I'm one of the Voice's angels!" I screamed at my tormentor. "And He...loves...me!"

Shapes and sounds blurred together as the vision faded.

95

CONSEQUENCES

Bright sunlight filtered through the shadows of tree branches and touched my face. The leaves were green, but not as green as they should be. The flowers, the creek, all the colors were dull. Even the air didn't smell as sweet as it once did.

I was propped against the trunk of a tree in the Garden. Gard sat in front of me and his face broke into a smile.

"You were fortunate I was able to heal you when I did."

I touched my head. There was a sharp pain at the back of my skull, then it was gone.

"What happened, Gard? Why didn't you meet me?"

The smile faded from Gard's face.

"The humans had yet to slay the Flock. I could have saved them both if Protex and Friend had not ambushed me. Our fight carried us into the forest. I thought I had slain Protex, but now I see he left to return to the humans. Friend kept it up until she, too, vanished." Gard sighed heavily. "Friend fought with her daggers and Protex fought with Hurrikiller's sword."

"Hurrikiller's *sword*? But I saw Kumpashin with it the day after the fight in Licemah!"

Gard raised his eyebrows. "What do you mean?"

"He said he was collecting weapons to give to you. That sword was in his hands."

Gard set his mouth in a thin line. "*Foster* was the one collecting weapons that day, not Kumpashin. It seems that one of the demons shapeshifted into his appearance and obtained the sword for Protex."

I closed my eyes. "If I was paying attention, I would've caught him."

"Do not blame yourself, Cair. Protex has the sword now. We need to figure out *why*. Why would he risk sneaking back into Licemah for it? Why is it important?"

Silence followed. When I opened my eyes again, the colors of the world were still dull, like someone had stolen the brightness away.

"What happened to the trees?" I asked Gard. "The colors are different."

"The humans have disobeyed the Voice. They killed the Spotless Flock. The consequences of their actions have fallen on Creation. Blueshade has returned to an imperfect state."

I put my head between my knees. "Not again. How could the Voice let this happen?"

Gard shook his head. "Did the Voice force the humans to slay the Flock? The demons may have influenced them, but the humans made the choice themselves."

"Where are the humans now?"

"Man, Woman and all their children have been banished from the Garden," Gard explained. "They are forbidden to return until one worthy human has been born among them. They must now grow their own food from the ground, or hunt for it."

"Hunt?"

"Because the humans have killed animals, some animals have developed a taste for meat. Lions hunt antelopes. Foxes hunt rabbits. Sharks hunt fish. There are now *predators* and *prey*. And as the humans have released death, they have also released sickness and disease. The Plague could shorten mankind's already shortened lifespan."

"*Lifespan*?"

Gard stared out over the pond. "Mankind is now mortal like all living things. If one makes it to one-hundred years of age, that will be the last year of his life."

I pushed myself from the tree. "That's worse than the consequences the demons had during the war. Will we wage a war on these humans, too?"

"The war has begun, but not by these humans," Gard said. "The demons want to take them from the Voice. Because of these new consequences, many humans will blame Him and turn away. They will seek their own way of life, just as the demons do. Our guidance is more important than ever."

I clenched my fists. "Where did Protex go?"

"He teleported," Gard continued, watching me. "Foster told me Protex has taken over your visions."

I grit my teeth together. "He did, but I think I know how to make him leave them."

I told Gard my plan.

"Cair, this is a *risky* plan," he said. "Are you sure you do not require help? *Because I have a strategy.* It involves..."

"That's okay, Gard. It'll work."

He stroked his chin, as if searching for an argument. His mouth opened and closed several times.

"Very well," he said at last. "Are you sure he won't see through your trick?"

"He won't. *Because I have a strategy.*"

18

MANSON'S WILL

Over the next hundred years, the conse-quences of Man and Woman's actions echoed through Creation. Banished from the Garden, they wandered across the Mainland and tried to find a new home. All of their children refused to take them in. Many blamed them for the extra work it took to farm vegetables and hunt animals. Mankind's white robes had become shredded and torn; they made new clothes with animal hides and plant fiber. Weighed down by harsh words and heartbreaks, Man and Woman's search turned into a bitter exile.

Then, they reached the eastern forest near the farm of their youngest child, Manson. When he saw them, he ran to his parents and welcomed them with open arms. He mourned with them over the life that was lost. Then, he helped them build a new one on his land.

Whenever other humans visited Manson, they would grumble and complain.

"Why do you look after *them*? Don't you know what they *did*?"

"Yes," Manson would reply. "But is there anything else you could say that would make them feel worse than they already do?"

As the sixth century passed, the humans got older. Their hair changed to gray before turning white. Wrinkles appeared on their skin and their movements became slower. The Plague didn't help either. This sickness would raise their body temperature and cause nausea and vomiting. For weeks the infected human would stay in bed, painfully waiting for the disease to pass.

In early-Spring of 700, Man and Woman were the first ones to die. Manson found them that cloudy morning still in bed with their arms wrapped around each other. The rest of the day passed with sweat and tears as Manson and his three sons dug graves in the ground. His wife and daughter anointed Man and Woman's heads with crowns of flowers. The men laid Man and Woman in the hard earth while I stood in the shadows of the trees and watched.

At sunset, I heard the rustle of wings as an angel landed next to me. I smiled the first smile I had all day as I embraced him.

"Gentull! How are y...*oh, too tight!*"

The burly angel relaxed his grip. "Sorry, Cair. Forgot my strength is back. A century in a hot spring does wonders, it does. 'Bout squeezed Incurajuh to pieces yesterday when she let me out."

"Are you okay?"

The jovialness in his eyes changed to something vacant and blank.

"Bit," Gentull admitted. "So much happened when I was there. Rather not talk about it. Oi, what say we talk about your book? Incurajuh said you were writin' one. D'you finish it?"

"It's here with me."

"Blimey! Ready to go, eh?"

The evening stars had come out by the time Manson had covered the graves with fresh earth. The family built a fire to keep warm in the chilly night air. Manson's wife brought dinner from the house, but he wouldn't eat. I observed Manson's children as they sat around the fire. His three sons had been born at the same time. Now, they were twenty-nine years old, with strong bodies that came from helping their father around the farm. Tern was the oldest, Gavin was the middle triplet and Miller was the youngest. The sister, Deanna, was only a year younger than her brothers; she was Manson's only daughter. All the humans had brown eyes, but sometimes I thought I saw a flicker of green in them.

After a few minutes, Gentull stepped out from the trees and held up a hand in greeting.

"Manson, favored by the Voice," he called out. "I come to you during this time of grief."

Miller took a step towards Gentull and pulled a knife from his belt. "Who are you?"

Tern grabbed his brother's arm. "It's an angel of the Voice. He's a friend."

"Oh, yeah, like the one who tricked Grandmother and Grandfather into ruining our world?" Miller spat. "How do we *know* he's a friend?"

"Because he fights for everything good," I answered and stood next to Gentull. My hands were held out in a gesture of peace. Miller shook off his brother's arm and turned away.

"The one who tricked Man and Woman," I continued. "He's one of the fallen angels that we call *demons*. These demons choose to follow their own ways and seek to destroy the Voice's goodness. But don't be afraid. The Voice will protect you, as long as you follow His ways."

Gavin slowly raised his hand into the air, as if he would break it if he moved too fast.

"Do you have a question, Gavin?"

Gavin coughed. "Yes, angel. How will He protect us?"

I pulled a large white-covered book from my robe and held it in front of me.

"This is the Sacred Book," I explained and handed it to Tern. "These words contain the truth of the world. It tells of the Voice, angels, demons and mankind. It gives examples on how to live and treat others. There are prophecies, genealogies and stories from the Lost Century as well."

Tern opened the book and started reading the first page. Deanna wiped her red eyes and looked over his shoulder. Their mother inclined her head at us.

"Thank you, angels," she whispered. "We will treasure this book for generations to come."

"I still don't get *how* this book will protect us," Miller said and rolled his eyes. "What do we do, throw it at the demons and hope it knocks them off their feet?"

"Peace, my son!" Manson shot Miller a sharp look. "They will not harm us!"

Miller threw his hands up in the air. He slouched into one of the roundhouses and kicked a rock on his way.

"Forgive my son. He wrestles with anger at the deaths of his grandparents."

Manson regarded us with his brown eyes. "What do you know of death, angels? For I fear my parents are only the first of the deaths to sweep this land."

I faltered as I tried to answer him. How could I put it into words?

"Death's hardest on those left behind," Gentull told him. "Your loved ones are gone. You look for them in the places they should be. They're not there. But the ache in your heart is."

Gentull put a hand on Manson's shoulder and smiled kindly. "Carry on in a way that'd make them proud. You'll see them again. When they've been faithful to the Voice, their souls go to God's Country."

Manson shuddered. "Mother and Father rebelled against the Voice. Are they really in God's Country after that?"

Gentull chuckled. "Which do you believe is stronger: your parents' failures, or the Voice's power to forgive those failures?"

"Father, look!"

Gavin was pointing at the graves. Two, white, transparent figures rose from the dirt. Deanna covered her mouth.

"Ghosts!" she screamed. "Father, look at the ghosts!"

Miller came barreling out of the roundhouse. He stopped short when he saw the figures rising up to the sky until they disappeared from view.

"See that?" Gentull asked and pointed at the sky. "The souls of your grandparents? They went to God's Country. Evil can't hurt them anymore."

Manson sighed in relief and collapsed into the arms of his wife.

"*Where* is God's Country?" Miller asked, with less scorn in his voice now.

I shook my head. "Only the Voice knows. Stay faithful to Him. Then, when you die, you will live in God's Country forever."

Manson cleared his throat and his wife helped him stand.

"My children, death will come for me soon. I want you to know my will for when that time comes."

All four children waited for him to continue speaking.

"Deanna, my only daughter, you will inherit your mother's cooking supplies. Some ingredients come from faraway lands. Your house will be filled with wonderful food and drink. Use them to bless those who go hungry."

Deanna clutched Miller's arm tightly and thanked her father. Her mother smiled.

"Miller, my son, you are headstrong and always do what needs to be done. Therefore, you will inherit our oxen. Use them to strengthen your farm and help your neighbors with heavy burdens they cannot bear alone."

The firelight flickered on Miller's face. "Thank you, Father."

Manson turned to Gavin. "Gavin, my son, maker of fences."

His family chuckled and Gavin blushed.

"You will inherit this land," Manson continued. "Your fences will keep good safe from evil."

Gavin, still blushing, looked at Tern who playfully slapped him on the back.

"And, finally, Tern," Manson said as he laced fingers with his wife. "Our firstborn, our eldest son. You have proven yourself capable of great things. I leave you with the Sacred Book in your hands."

Tern looked down at the book and then back up at his father. Gratitude shone on his face.

His mother glanced at her roundhouse. "My son, you'll have something from me as well. I'll give you the rings that your grandmother passed to me before her death. These are the rings made by the Voice for her wedding. They're almost two-hundred years old! When you marry, you can give them to your wife."

Tern grinned and threw his arms around his parents.

"Thank you both," he said as they rubbed his head.

Tern rejoined his siblings as Manson spoke again. "The world is changing. More and more people are using gold to purchase goods and services. When I die, you will divide my gold evenly. It is in a sack under our bed. Use it wisely. Treat each other right and follow the Voice and His ways. I love you all."

After the children embraced their father, the humans thanked us again and put out their fire. We watched them go into their roundhouses.

Gentull sighed.

"Family. Community. That's what those bat-wings want to destroy."

I glanced up at the twinkling stars. Somewhere past them was God's Country. Zafe, Cuverr, Laff and dozens more angels were welcoming Man and Woman into their forever home. A land without pain, sorrow or suffering. God's Country was rumored to be more beautiful than Blueshade was before the war. A place all could enjoy and their sins against God be forgiven.

But that was the troubling thought. If men could be redeemed, couldn't the demons be, too?

ANGEL OF JOKES

Manson was right. Blueshade was filled with cries of grieving people as more humans died days later. We angels flew between the remaining humans and gave them encouragement and comfort. Gard showed them how to use the Link, so they could speak directly to the Voice. Securitie encouraged after-burial feasts where the living shared memories of the dead around the table. Kumpashin even taught humans the song we sang over our dead:

> *"Sleep well, you have earned your rest,*
> *Sleep well, away from every stress,*
> *Sleep well, your love remains to shine,*
> *Sleep well, in the hearts you've left behind."*

It sounded strange, the humans singing our song. They called it "The Death Song". I don't know what I would've named it, but it wouldn't be "The Death Song". The tune caught like fire and became popular across the three continents. Death was now as common as birth. It made many humans realize how short life was. They eagerly read their Sacred Books. Words on paper were memorized. Whenever one human was sad, another would recite words from the Sacred Book related to that feeling. In this way, the humans reassured each other.

As Securitie put it, they grumbled less and smiled more.

Thirteen years after his parents, Manson died. He had looked forward to it, because he would be with his wife again, who'd died two years earlier.

Only Tern and Gavin came to bury their father. They'd been living their own lives and both were leaders in their communities. Tern's community lived in stone houses on the shoreline of the western sea. Gavin's community dwelled in wood houses under the shade of a giant banyan tree near the Frost River. When the brothers returned to their childhood home, I could see the same confidence in their strides.

They buried Manson between his parents and his wife. They spent the night weeping together. In the morning, the brothers bathed and changed their clothes. It was now time to carry out the words Manson had spoken to them long ago.

I flew down to serve as a witness. The three of us stood in the warm interior of Manson's roundhouse. The fire from this morning's breakfast had died; wisps of smoke escaped through the tiny hole in the roof.

"They should've been here," Tern grumbled as he dragged a wooden box from underneath his parents' bed. "I sent word to them four days ago."

Gavin shrugged. "Maybe they're way up in the desert. You know how much our siblings like traveling." He looked at me. "Have you seen them, angel? I mean, I know you can fly and stuff."

"I can fly. What's this *stuff* you speak of?"

"I guess *stuff* is another word I use for things. Objects. Items. Just one less syllable."

Before I could reply, Tern cried out in distress.

"Look!" He lifted the box upside down. "Gone! Everything's gone!"

It was true. The gold, the rings, all of it had disappeared.

At that moment, there was a loud crash as the wattle wall exploded. I shielded the humans with my wings. Woven wood flew everywhere. When the dust settled, Securitie stood in the opening.

"Oops," she said and grinned sheepishly. "This house wasn't as strong as I thought it'd be."

She stepped inside. Enérgeia swirled in her hands. The mud, straw, and wattle flew through the air and settled back in place. She turned from the wall and beamed at the shocked brothers.

"Good as new! You must be Tern and Gavin. I'm Securitie."

Gavin recovered first. "Securitie? Oh, I've heard about you! The women in my community call you the Angel of Jokes, because you make them laugh."

Securitie threw back her head and laughed.

"*Angel of Jokes?* Wow, I've never been called *that* before! But, yes. I do like to laugh."

I smiled. "Why are you here, Sec?"

"Why *am* I here? Well, um...oh!"

An anxious expression replaced her smile. She shook her red curls.

"Cair! You're the closest angel I could find! There's something happening on the Frost River! A group of humans are being attacked by dinosaurs!"

She glanced at the wide-eyed brothers.

"*Their* siblings are in this group of humans being attacked by dinosaurs!"

The brothers gasped in surprise.

"Sec," I said firmly. "What kind of dinosaurs?"

She flapped her arms. "The flying ones."

"Then, let's go!"

We were almost out the doorway when Tern called to me.

"Angel?" He still clutched the box. "Can you let us know what happens?"

"By the Voice," I promised him. "I'll return as soon as I can."

20

THEFT

A small village had sprung up on the eastern shore of the Frost River. Three wooden docks had been built to harbor boats. A bigger boat designed to ferry people across the river dwarfed the others.

However, it was to the western bank we flew. Five humans stumbled through the shallows toward a fifty-foot boat called a *ship*. It had rounded hulls and curved sterns. Three flying creatures wheeled in the sky above the humans.

"Icedactyls!" I exclaimed as we closed the distance. "Icedactyls are after them!"

The first human made it to the ship. He darted to the giant post in the center and let down the rectangular sail. He waved furiously at the others. An icedactyl shrieked and dove toward another man at the back of the group. It yanked him from the water. The man beat back its sharp beak with his fists. The dinosaur dropped him almost immediately. The man died instantly when he landed on a dead tree half in the water. The creature clicked its beak and dove for another human.

Those teeth were solid ice. Icedactyls usually hunted fish. Why were they going after the humans? I was close, but not close enough to save the screaming woman as the icedactyl swooped down on her.

The second man had reached the ship. He turned around and threw the spear in his hand. It shot through the air and pierced the dinosaur in the stomach. It shrieked and dropped into the sand. The flailing wings knocked the woman over and the man behind her helped her back up.

Miller and Deanna, I realized.

The second man helped the siblings onto the ship. They hunkered down on the quarterdeck as he ran back for his spear. The two remaining icedactyls converged upon him. Their beaks snapped into his body and he started screaming.

The enérgeia shot from my hands. It swirled around the icedactyls and froze them completely. The dinosaurs were the same height as me. Their leathery wings reminded me of those the demons had. Icy teeth that had been knocked out during the fight were already starting to regrow inside the three-foot long beaks. A dark blue color tinted their pebbly skin.

The icedactyls collapsed in the sand into a sudden sleep. But the man wasn't as fortunate.

We landed next to him. Securitie covered her mouth in horror.

My enérgeia faded as I lowered my hands. As I glanced at the ship, I saw the first man was at the oar-like blade on the left side. The ship made a grinding sound as he pushed it away from shore. Wind filled the rectangle sail as it carried the boat away into the ocean.

Securitie looked confused. "Wait, aren't they going to bury them first?"

My voice trembled as I answered her. "How could they just *leave* them there? Sec, can you...?"

Her voice sounded small. "Sure."

I left Securitie on shore to bury the two men. Before the ship made it out to deep water, I landed hard on the deck. The first man cowered down behind his oar and Deanna dropped to her knees. Only Miller remained standing.

"Oh, it's the angel," he snorted. "Why are *you* here?"

"*I* am here, Miller, because *you* lack respect for your fellow man."

I looked back at the shrinking coastline. "Why haven't you buried those who have died?"

Miller shrugged. "Oh, those other two? Maybe because I was *running* from those flying dinosaurs chasing me!"

"We were fine until you started waving those rings around," the other man muttered.

Miller rolled his eyes. "Captain, I didn't pay you for your opinion."

I kept my wings extended and took a step towards him.

"Do you know that your father is dead? That your brothers wonder why you weren't there to bury him?"

Deanna's lip trembled and a single tear fell into her lap. Miller only shrugged his shoulders.

"So, what? I've already got my inheritance," Miller said. He pointed at the bag his sister carried. "I stole the gold before my brothers could get to the house. Most of it spent on the captain and his boat, but there's still some left. I took the rings, too."

The bluntness of his confession startled me.

"I showed them the rings on the way to the boat," Miller continued with a smug smile. "They were *very* impressed. Then those dinosaurs showed up and tried to kill us!"

"What were you thinking?" I clapped my hand to my forehead. "Those dinosaurs hunt fish! Shiny fish! Of course, the rings would attract them!"

Deanna and the captain both trembled under my furious stare. Miller only threw up his hands.

"How was I supposed to know *that*? We first tried running through the water, but Deanna tripped. We lost three of the rings to the current. At least we still have two of them!"

My body started glowing with light. "You'd know that if you'd been reading your Sacred Book! You'd also know that stealing is wrong!"

Miller turned his back on me. "*And?* You can't hurt me. You're supposed to protect me and all my kin. Go away and leave me alone."

The light faded from my body. I felt drained, defeated.

"You don't have to stay with him," I called out to the other two humans. "You don't have share in his consequences."

The captain rose to his feet. He grunted and patted the sack tied to his belt. I heard the clink of gold coins.

Deanna brushed her raven hair aside and looked up at me with conflicted eyes. I saw the same shade of green in them that was in Woman's eyes all those years ago.

"I...*can't*," Deanna said quietly. "I love him, angel."

She reached out her trembling hand and her brother took it. He pulled her up and she nestled against his side. Miller faced me again. The green shade in his eyes was darker than his sister's.

21

GREEN SHADE

Tern shook his head. "I can't believe our own brother would steal from us! Where did you say they went again?"

"The captain took them to Bacaniber Island," I admitted. "Bacaniber gave them shelter."

"I still can't get over why our sister would stay with him," Tern said. "If he ever hurts her..."

"Miller makes a lot of wrong choices," Gavin said to him. "But he wouldn't hurt Deanna."

Tern inclined his head in my direction. "Thank you, angel, for coming back."

Gavin sighed and hefted his haversack on his shoulders. He glanced back at what used to be Manson's farm. The other family was herding their livestock inside the fence. Gavin sold his inheritance so he and Tern would get some of the gold back.

Gavin hugged his brother. "Come visit in late-Spring. Our tree will have green leaves again."

Tern laughed. "Then you can follow me home for early-Summer and try fishing from the sea."

The brothers parted ways. It amazed me how they were able to move on with their lives and not seek out Miller in vengeance. Maybe there was still hope for humanity after all.

The years rushed along. Tern's community on the west coast continued to thrive. The ten stone houses expanded to twenty-five. Fishermen fished the waters for anchovies, sardines and sea bass. Six docks formed a decent harbor for their boats. Tern eventually became the mayor of the settlement. His daughter Yaz was born in 735. She had inherited her great-grandmother's dark curly hair.

Gavin's community flourished as well. The eighteen wooden houses were nestled under the biggest banyan tree in Blueshade. Dozens of prop roots grew straight into the ground, giving the impression of a grove instead of a single tree. The community traded lumber with the people who lived in the eastern desert. In return, they received gold to make coins. Gavin, too, had a daughter born three years after Tern's.

Miller and Deanna were doing fairly well on Bacaniber Island. Bacaniber adopted them into his tribe. Miller and Deanna had long since been married. They started a family: twins, a boy and a girl. Out of all the humans left, only Deanna was able to produce children with skins of different colors.

I visited Incurajuh one day. We sat on the roof of one of the grass huts. Below us, the Bacaniber were preparing a feast; fruit, fish and crab legs. A rare tideicthy had been caught in their nets the night before. This dolphin-like dinosaur, roasting on the spit, would become the main course. A special feast for the new year.

"Hard to believe we've been alive for seven-hundred and forty-four years," I told Incurajuh.

"Seven-hundred and forty-five, starting tomorrow," she said. "And these humans only live one-hundred years maybe. You know, I tried explaining how old we are to them, but it goes over their heads."

A group of children chased each other down the beach. I spotted Katrina instantly. Her pale color stood out among the darker-skinned Bacanibers. Her twin brother Darnol, on the other hand, was as dark as the other children. They yelled and giggled as they sloshed through a tidal pool.

I sighed. "Incurajuh, what do you think about this green shade in their eyes? I know they've always had it, but lately it's getting bigger."

"The green shade is *everywhere*. When Man and Woman took Protex's hands, he led them away from the Voice. The green shade represents *sin,* the immoral act against the Voice's ways. The green shade has passed on to all their children as well."

An old woman sat in a wooden chair by the firepit with a Sacred Book open on her lap. The green shade in her eyes was nearly invisible, a speck in the corner of her pupil. A young man stalked fish in the shallows with a spear. He jabbed it down into the waves. When the spear came up empty, the green shade in his eyes flared and he slapped the water in frustration.

"But why now? Why is the shade more apparent in their eyes?"

"Because the demons are trying to take humans away from the Voice," Incurajuh answered. "Miller is already astray. There he is, down there."

Several men sharpened their spears for the next hunt. Miller talked to each of them. A wide grin spread across his face as he let them pass his two rings around. One ring had a diamond, the other a pearl. One of the men refused to hold the rings and went back to sharpening his spear. Miller only laughed and went over to the firepit to show off his rings some more. The man glared after him with angry eyes.

"He should be watchful of that one," Incurajuh whispered. "That is Bacaniber II, Bacaniber's son. He has not liked Miller since the day he arrived. Anger leads to hate. We know what hate can do to the world."

"You're right about the green shade, though. It's like a parasite leeching off mankind. They can't see it. They don't even know it exists. And *that*'s what's concerning."

I thought of Man and Woman wandering the land homeless. Of the hurt in Tern's eyes when his brother and sister weren't at their father's funeral. Of Miller's outright approval of stealing from his family. How many other similar things were happening across Blueshade?

I stood up suddenly and unfurled my wings.

Incurajuh put her hand on my robe. "Cair, what is wrong?"

The villagers below looked up at me in awe. My seven-foot shadow must've been impressive against the sunlight.

"When I leave, have them start reading their Sacred Books," I told a wide-eyed Incurajuh. "Protex *will* tell me what he's planning. *I'm* taking the fight to *him*."

22

WHEN THE WALL
FELL

The clouds hid the moon and stars on this snowy night. An army of giants, dragons and wolves stalked up the ridge towards the city of Licemah. Two demons peeled off from the main force. They crept through a patch of pine trees and stopped just outside the shimmering yellow wall that surrounded the city.

"'S make this quick," Protex grunted and brushed snow from his hair. "Want to be there when the giants smash the barricade."

"Oh, this'll take no time at all," Sage replied. She unscrewed the small jar she carried. A being with black sludgy skin emerged from inside. Its red eyes glared at the wall.

"Neutralize it, now!" Sage commanded.

The Shadow slithered into the wall.

"More!" Sage shouted. Dozens of Shadows left the jar and disappeared into the wall. The dark yellow flickered and opened up a space in the wall. Sage walked through. Protex started to follow her, but she kicked him hard. He fell back into the snow as the wall resealed itself.

"'S *that* for?" Protex snarled as he leaped from the frozen ground.

From the other side of the transparent wall, Sage looked like she was entirely yellow.

"Sorry, Protex. Looks like *I'm* the one who'll bring Cuverr to Hurrikiller."

"We were supposed to do it together!" Protex hissed.

Sage tilted her head to the side. Then she laughed.

"Return to the army, Protex. Kynd's there, right? That's where *you* want to be anyway."

She unsheathed Hurrikiller's sword. "Aw, I *love* this blade!"

She ran off between the stone buildings. Protex roared and shot flames at the wall. They seared against it, but they didn't burn through. Protex collapsed to the ground in defeat. The flames vanished, leaving trails of smoke behind.

"Congratulations, Cair," Protex stumbled to his feet. He faced the pine tree I'd been leaning against this whole time. "Learned to control your visions, did you?"

"What are you going to do with the humans?"

The demon smirked. "The humans, eh? That what you're worried about? Why bring us to this *particular* memory?"

Yellow enérgeia in the form of a whip slithered from my right hand. "The humans, Protex!"

"Not saying anything, Cair."

I threw the whip forward. It coiled around him like a snake and bound him tight. The tail end wrapped around his mouth. I heard muffled sounds from behind his gag. He glared at me with narrow eyes but I glared right back.

"Then don't say anything at all."

Angels flew back and forth over the city as they prepared for battle. They didn't pay me any attention. I flew directly to the quarters. My heart ached as I crept up the stairs and past the rooms that used to be our resting places.

I stopped by my room. I heard an angel screaming at Hurrikiller from inside.

"I crawled through the mud! You just stood there, watching me crawl!"

A single tear dripped from my eye.

"I reached my hand out to you..."

"No! Y-you let me crawl through the mud, like y-you let me crawl through this war!"

Time froze as I walked into my room. I brushed past a still Hurrikiller. A few feet away stood the Cair from the past. She was sobbing, too. The fire scroll dangled from one of her hands. I longed to comfort her, but there was something else I needed to do. The words Gard spoke in the Swamp of Darkness came back to me:

"If someone had committed evil in their first life, would you say they could find redemption in their second or third?"

I forced myself to look at him. His tortured face was immobile, his yellow eyes locked on Cair.

"Hurr, I know you can hear me. You *will* die. But you'll live again. Please...*please*..."

I blinked through my tears. "...repent...when you come back...ask forgiveness because I...forgive you..."

The last three words were the hardest to say. But they broke through the wall inside and rushed around my heart. The compassion from the Voice rose up to meet them. It felt like a broken bowl being repaired. I still felt the cracks and they hurt when I touched them. But they were no longer scattered.

A wheezing sound came from the hallway. I wiped my eyes on my sleeve and took one last look at Hurrikiller. Bumps marred his once-perfect face. His yellow eyes still stared at the Cair from the past. I remembered when they use to be green.

"Goodbye, Hurr," I whispered and walked from the room.

Protex leaned on the doorway for support. My rope still wrapped around him, though the tail was shorter, like it had been bitten through. The demon finally caught his breath.

"'S why you're here? To love what you've lost?"

"We *both* lost loved ones this night," I told him. His glare no longer had any power over me. He noticed it, too, and stared sullenly at the stone floor.

"You really believe the Voice would redeem demons like us? After all we've done to His precious world? 'S foolish thinking. Kynd is *dead*. Can't bring her back. But when I die, I'll bring her news of what I've done. Mankind will remember my name with fear."

I raised my hands. "Then you've already lost."

He shut his eyes against the bright light that filled the quarters.

"Protex," I raised my voice. "You are condemned by your own words."

The stone beneath our feet started to crack.

"I don't fear you any longer."

Protex fell sideways as the room swirled with yellow words. Words that came from the pages of the Sacred Books.

"You're not welcome in my mind. You-...cannot...return!"

He disappeared beneath the shattered floor.

THE SECOND REALM

"How does it feel winning your battle?" Securitie asked me.

"*Amazing*. A week into this new year, and he's left me alone."

"That's great, Cair! Oh, hold on a second…"

She rose from her purple-orange rug to address one of the nearby humans.

"Hey, there! I have a joke for you. Actually, *two* jokes. Here's the first one: Why was six afraid of seven?"

The wizened old man scratched his head. "Hmm, I don't know, angel. Why *was* six afraid of seven?"

"Because seven ate nine!" Securitie threw back her head in joyful laughter. The man chuckled.

"That was a good one, angel!"

"Here's the next one: Why was nine the last number eaten by seven?"

The man thought for a minute, then shrugged his narrow shoulders. "Because seven was full?"

"Because seven couldn't swallow tin! Get it? You can't *eat* tin!"

"Ah, yes, because *ten* and *tin* sound the same, but mean different things."

The man wandered over to some other humans sitting under a raised tent. He eagerly began telling them the jokes.

I looked past them. Sand dunes stretched out in every direction and the sun shimmered overhead. The humans sat on long rugs inside the tents. They talked and laughed with one another. Some nibbled on the remnants of the meal: nuts, melons, mutton and rice cakes. These desert dwellers wore light clothing that hid their tanned olive skin. Herds of sheep grazed on scattered tufts of grass nearby. The wind whistled mournfully.

But the people were smiling. For today, these desert dwellers had become the Second Realm of Men. And their Guardian Angel waddled over with the sun shining on his bald head.

"What a great gift!" Foster showed us a necklace made out of snail shells. He set it in Securitie's palm.

"Seems the Aidarians like you," she said as she examined the shells closely.

"Aidaria, she's a real sweetheart. She hopes to find a spot to build a city."

I glanced over at the elderly woman whose red hair was tied in an elegant bun. A green snake and three stars decorated a huge flag which hung over her tent. She was laughing at the wizened man's jokes, causing her eyes to crinkle.

I nudged Securitie. "Aidaria looks just like you, Sec."

Securitie chuckled. "If I ever needed to look like a human, I'd change in to her alright!"

"Transformation isn't unheard of," Foster said as he took back his necklace. "Speaking of transformation, the way you banished Protex from you mind, Cair, was phenomenal! And drawing support from the words of the Sacred Books? Well played."

"Thanks, Foster. But I still don't know what he's planning to do to the humans."

Foster waved his hand around at the surrounding tents. "Take the victories where you can. Come on, you just defeated Protex in psychological warfare! *That* is something to be proud of. Oh, and on a completely unrelated matter, would you mind bringing me a cup of that tea stuff? I can't drink it, but it would help my credentials as their Guardian Angel."

Tea was a new drink crafted by Gavin's people. They harvested tea plants and mixed them with water to make a satisfying alternative to milk, water and juice. Just like Bale's scrolls prospered his people, tea prospered Gavin's. The Aidarians sold their abundant sheep to get crates of this new drink.

I was carrying a cup back to Foster when I bumped into the wizened man. He landed hard on his bottom. The cup thudded into the sand and the tea spilled out into a black puddle.

"I'm sorry," I apologized and reached out my hand. "Let me help you..."

The man was gone. In his place was a strange creature that looked like a dinosaur and a monkey mixed together. My arm dropped.

"Sheeld?"

The creature leaped to his feet and hissed. The people closest to us cried out and retreated into their tents.

"Sheeld?" I repeated. "What are *you* doing here?"

With sudden speed, he charged past me and loped out into the desert.

I unfurled my wings just as Foster and Securitie joined me.

"Was that a mirage? I thought I just saw Sheeld," Foster gazed at the dwindling figure.

"He was the old man Sec was telling jokes to."

Securitie's mouth hung open. "You mean, I was telling jokes to a *demon?*"

Foster tapped his beaky nose. "Okay, Cair, so how about you go after him, and I stay with my peeps?"

"Peeps?"

"It means 'people'. Made-up words, you know."

"Yeah, you do that," I muttered. "Come on, Sec!"

I launched into the air with Securitie close behind me.

24

LONG TIME, NO SEE

Sheeld was running west across the desert, using his three-clawed feet and five-clawed knuckles. His red-and-green body was easy to see against the yellow sand. He sped towards the looming foothills of the Glacier Mountains. We'd lose him if he reached the trees.

I summoned a massive ball of enérgeia and hurled it as far as I could. It exploded on the ground ten feet ahead of him. Sheeld was knocked off his feet. He sneezed, blinded by the grains of falling sand. By the time he regained his balance, I had landed nearby. A glowing yellow cage floated down from the sky and trapped him inside it. Securitie hovered overhead, the cage connected to the enérgeia from her hands. Her wings put her down next to me.

Sheeld rammed against the bars.

"Let me go! I ain't done nothin'!"

The third hand on his tail was trying to push against the roof of the cage.

"Where have *you* been?" Securitie asked. "Long time, no see!"

Sheeld curled his lip. "I been tryin' to not stay stuck in this body you gave me!"

Securitie's face reddened. "Oh, sorry. I didn't know you'd have it *this* long. At least you can still shapeshift."

A deep purr rumbled in the demon's throat. "I like these human bodies. Better than a frog or a rabbit. Almost got eaten by a bird one time."

"Don't change the subject," I said. "Why were you at the humans' ceremony?"

"Scoutin'," he continued in his deep voice. "I'ma hand it to you, Cair, you puttin' a hurt on us with those Sacred Books. Feels like runnin' into walls when we try hittin' 'em."

"Good, because the humans belong to the Voice."

Securitie's arms wavered. "Hey, Cair? I can't hold this cage for much longer."

"Alright, Sheeld, let's make this quick. Tell me what Protex is after."

Sheeld tugged on his snout. "How 'bout I tell you what Protex is after, and *then* you let me go? I swear by the Voice."

Securitie gasped and her hands dropped. The cage disappeared. Sheeld sighed and stretched his long tail. But he stayed where he was.

"Swearing by the Voice is a serious oath," I told him.

The third hand on his tail started scratching his back. He nodded with eyes half-closed.

"It's serious, all right. If it's serious, that means I can't break it. If I *do* break it, that means I'll die on the spot. I ain't gonna lie to you, 'cause I like livin'."

"He has a point," Securitie admitted.

I started pacing in front of the demon. "Fine. By the Voice, I'll let you go once you've told me what Protex is up to."

Sheeld yawned. "Protex always liked the Shadows. After Lord Hurrikiller died, Protex claimed their obedience before Sage could. All these years, he tried goin' after her with the Shadows. Sage was too strong for him. Now, lookie what happens next. The Voice makes these *humans* with flesh and bone bodies. They kill the Spotless Flock. Now, they with Him and *not* with Him at the same time. Like, uh...*hopeful, green-eyed sinners*. You seen it, ain't you, Cair?"

There was a pause as he licked his chops. I knew he meant the *sin* in their eyes.

Securitie pointed a finger at him. "You said it like you're planning to eat them!"

Sheeld bent over and stretched his arms out on the sand. "Oh, I ain't gonna eat 'em! *Sin* is somethin' the Shadows eat. As soon as a human sins, then the Shadow can take over the body. Protex thinks he can beat Sage with Shadow-controlled humans."

I stared at him in disbelief. "But if *that's* true, then he's desperate."

"*Very desperate*," Sheeld agreed. "Kunsiderut's dead, and Kunsern joined our side. Friend's his only demon left, but it won't be long 'til she's with us. Protex's gonna mix the Shadows with humans. A whole bunch at once."

I stopped pacing as the image of the twin-snake blade flashed through my mind. "A whole bunch at once?"

"Protex wants to cover Blueshade with this army," Sheeld continued. "Then see what the Voice does about it."

"He'd restore the world again like He did before," Securitie said. "And maybe get *you* out of that dinosaur-monkey body if you repent!"

Sheeld slammed a fist into the ground and sand flew everywhere.

"Lord Hurrikiller's comin' back, Gard said so himself! If he said so himself, *that* means Hurrikiller's gonna defeat the Voice. If Hurrikiller's gonna defeat the Voice, *that* means..."

"...you won't have to repent," I finished for him. "Back to the humans. How exactly does Protex plan to use them as his army? Sage would only annihilate them."

The demon scratched his face with the claws on his hind leg. "Protex wants to hurt Sage. But he wants to hurt the Voice *more*. What better way than having His humans kill each other? Humans fightin' their kinfolk? Good place to start."

I looked straight into his eyes. "When?"

"They gonna do it tonight."

"Where?"

25

WAITING

The sea brushed under the wooden docks and rocked the boats moored to them. The night winds caressed the fire in the braziers and cast shadows on the twenty-five stone houses. We perched on the unfinished roof of the twenty-sixth. This building was taller than all the others.

"Those Shadow thingies better watch out," Gentull grunted. He hoisted the golden war-hammer up on his burly shoulders. "Won't get me this time."

Gard stooped next to him. "It is good to have you back, my brother. However, I do understand if you wanted to sit this one out."

"What, and miss all the fun?" Gentull laughed. "Incurajuh and Foster are bound to their realms. You'll need all the help you can get."

"I'll help you as long as there aren't, like, any *bugs*," Kumpashin said.

"I doubt there will be any insects tonight, Kumpashin," Gard reassured him. The teacher angel was focused on the path that led out of town and into the forest. "Did you warn the humans, Cair?"

"Hours ago. I also gave them some of the golden weapons we scavenged from Licemah."

I remembered Tern's face as he thanked me and distributed the weapons among his people. Some of his carpenters had constructed something called a *door*. It was a barrier placed on two hinges that made it swing back and forth. The door covered one of the buildings where all the women and children were sleeping tonight. Tern's wife and ten-year-old daughter Yaz were there.

"Very good." Gard continued. "Did Sheeld provide you with any other details?"

"Nope," Securitie answered him. She thrusted her golden staff like she was jabbing imaginary foes. "Once he gave us the when and where, we released him."

Gard acknowledged her response with a wave of her hand. He crossed to the other side of the roof and resumed his watch.

Securitie jabbed the staff near Kumpashin, who pushed it away. "Could you stop moving? Protex will see you swinging that thing around."

"No, he won't," Securitie huffed back. "Ooh, I made up another joke today! I'll say 'Knock, knock', then you say 'Who's there?'. I'll say a word, then you say my word and 'who' and *then* I'll say the punchline! It's called a knock-knock joke."

Kumpashin put a hand to his head. "A joke before battle? Like, seriously?"

"Go on, out with it then," Gentull said and smiled.

"Knock, knock."

"Who's there?" Gentull asked.

"Mustache." Securitie put her finger on her upper lip.

"Mustache who?"

"Mustache you a question, but I'll shave it for later!"

She dropped her finger. Gentull guffawed and Kumpashin nodded his head.

"Clever, because some humans shave their mustaches. I think I get it."

I crossed the roof to where Gard continued his watch.

"Do you see anything?" I asked.

"A few men peeping from their window-holes. But nothing new."

"Gard, remember one of my past visions? The one where Hurrikiller gave Sheeld a leather pouch? I forgot to ask Sheeld about that while the oath trapped him."

"Fear not, Cair. The information Sheeld *did* provide you with is invaluable. Because of it, we are here to prevent Protex from carrying out his terrible plan. After this, we can find Sheeld again. It appears this leather pouch is connected to Hurrikiller's next resurrection."

He sighed. "Let us not worry about tomorrow, but instead entrust it to the Voice. He..."

Gentull slouched over and Gard fell silent at the hard look in his eyes.

"He's here," Gentull whispered. "Down by the docks."

We all crept to the west side of the roof and peered over it. Protex stood alone on the beach. He kicked a log from one of the humans' campfires. Then, he knelt down and started drawing lines in the sand. The moonlight seemed to darken his red hair to the color of blood. A sword was sheathed in the hilt hanging from his belt, the flames from the nearest brazier flickering on its twin-snake hilt.

"So, boss, what's the plan?" Kumpashin glanced at Gard. "You know it's a trap, right?"

"I am not anyone's boss, Kumpashin. But I do agree this is a trap."

"'Course, you're our leader," Gentull said. "It's okay to admit it."

"Well, I..." Gard faltered.

"Yeah," Securitie chimed in. "Like the fight in Licemah. You rallied us."

"I didn't do *that* much..."

"We know you as the humblest angel of us all," I reminded him. "Give yourself *some* credit. The Voice chose *you* to lead us tonight. No matter what happens."

The rest of us looked at him expectantly. He cleared his throat like he always did before he gave a speech. Then, he just smiled.

"Thank you for the encouragement. You are right of course."

"So, boss," Kumpashin repeated. "What's the plan?"

26

FIGHT BY THE SEA

Gard, Gentull and I had surrounded Protex. The demon finished scribbling in the sand and rose to his feet. After quick glances at the other two angels, Protex settled his yellow eyes on me.

"Hello, Cair. Looks like you've found me. Even came prepared."

"You are past the point of repentance," Gard said. He gripped the hilt of his sword. "You have made that clear with your words and actions. For your crimes against the Voice and His Creation, you are sentenced to death."

The demon shrugged. "If that's what it takes to see Kynd again."

I saw the desperation in his eyes. He was beyond reason. Strange to think of him as my tormenter for such a long time. Crackling black lightning bolts formed in his open hands. Protex unfurled his scaly wings and lifted off the ground. He hovered twenty feet in the air and flung the bolts down at us.

Gentull knocked one into the sand with his war-hammer. Gard dodged the one aimed at him. His own wings extended and he shot up into the sky. Protex tried summoning another one, but Gard was on him. He slashed at the demon's arm and left a red line across it. Protex sent Gard through the air with a well-aimed kick. I was ready to leap off the ground and go after him when I heard Gentull bellow behind me.

Another demon was fighting him. It was Friend, Protex's last ally. Her squat form enabled her to dance around the weighted swings of Gentull's war-hammer. Gentull spent more energy lifting his weapon from the ground than he did swinging it. She darted in with her dagger and left wounds in several places.

"I'm leavin' holes in ya!" Friend taunted in her whiny nasal voice.

Gentull stumbled forward when she ran her dagger between his shoulder blades. He dropped to his knees. Friend twirled her dagger as she leaped on him again. Or *tried* to leap on him again. My enérgeia took the form of a war-hammer and slammed into her side. She whined as the impact sent her higher and higher until she landed out in the sea.

Gentull spit sand from his mouth. "Little bat-wing!"

The swirling yellow hammer evaporated and I pulled Gentull to his feet. Gard and Protex had moved their fight into the woods. Flashes of black and yellow through the trees were all I could see of them.

The glimmer of torchlight from the town caught my eyes. Men armed with golden weapons had come out from their houses. And three-hundred Shadows swirled in the sky above them like a crazy storm cloud.

Tern led the group of men. At seventy-eight years old, he possessed strength and energy of a man half his age. Tern jabbed his golden sword at a swooping Shadow. On contact, the shrieking creature disappeared. But more kept diving. The men stayed close to each other in a tight cluster.

One man with short brown hair staggered from the group. He stood tall, dropped his golden axe and raised his hands skyward. One of the Shadows swooped down and vanished into his body. His eyes were now completely green. He bared his teeth in a feral smile, picked up his axe and swung it at another man in the group.

"No!" I screamed as I shot toward them. Two dozen Shadows met me and reached out with their long, curled fingers. My golden sword cut four of them down. The rest would've devoured me if the other angels hadn't been there. Flashes of a yellow staff, whip and war-hammer glowed through the black mass of wailing mouths. After another minute of swinging and dodging, we killed all those Shadows.

Kumpashin and Gentull charged into the main mass of Shadows. I started after them, then I collapsed in the sand. Securitie flew down next to me.

"Cair, what's wrong?"

"My arms."

"I think you're not used to the sword-swinging," she said and placed her hands on my arms. Her healing enérgeia soothed the fatigue.

"Thanks, Sec."

I found Tern in the fray. He was climbing the steps to the roof of the unfinished building. Five men were beside him. Each had a weapon raised over his head. Together, the weapons formed a golden barrier. Many Shadows dove at it, but they all changed course before they could touch it. Tern encouraged his men forward. He and four others kept the golden barrier raised while the fifth man dropped to a knee. He fit an arrow to his bow and took aim. The arrow shot down at an incline and dropped one of the men with green eyes.

One of the men, I thought sadly.

The fight on the ground was getting worse. Shadow after Shadow slipped into the humans who stumbled from the group. The green shade filled their entire eyes as the Shadow-led humans turned on their fellows. Six bodies littered the ground.

Securitie shook my shoulder urgently. "Cair, let's go!"

She shot off toward the hut where the women and children were. I unfolded my wings and followed behind her. Friend had returned. The squat demon chortled as she sliced into the door with her dagger. Screams came from behind it.

Securitie slammed into her at full speed. Friend whined as she was catapulted through the thatch roof of the next house over. The roof caved in and Friend burst through the stone wall, covered in dust.

"Ya too late!" Friend spat on the ground.

The hinges creaked and the door swung open. I watched in horror as eleven of the women marched out of the house as if in a trance. Some held forks and some held knives. One even carried a small pot sloshing with boiling water. But each woman had green eyes.

Enérgeia shot from my hands in the forms of ropes. They circled Friend and pinned her arms to her side. The dagger dropped from her hand. She whined as the ropes dragged her to me.

I looked over my shoulder. The women continued their steps toward the fighting men.

"Sec!"

"On it!"

Securitie gained altitude as she flew upwards. By the time the women had reached the men, she came down like an arrow. She pressed her hands forward, ready to release her enérgeia. Suddenly, her body crumpled against an invisible barrier. Her arms and wings spread out in different directions. Her mouth opened in shock as she fell.

"Sec!" I screamed. Her sudden fall had distracted me from Friend, who jumped straight into the air. She twisted her body into the ropes and yanked me off my feet. Two, sharp pains came soon after; one on my left knee, one on my back. My concentration broke and the enérgeia left me.

"What's wrong with ya, bird-wing?" Friend hissed in my ear. "Ya look so sad!"

I tried shoving her off, but she held me down.

A whoosh of wind, Friend's sudden yelp of surprise, her weight off of me...

"And *you* look comical."

Kumpashin's eyes followed Friend's tumbling body as she sailed over the trees and into the forest.

27

PROTEX'S REVENGE

I followed Kumpashin back into battle. Directly over the unfinished building, Gentull and Gard fought against maybe thirty or forty Shadows. Their presence prevented the foul creatures from diving on Tern's archer, who still shot from the rooftop. A mass of green-eyed men and women clogged the stairs, trying to get up to the archer. Tern and the four others blocked the way and swung at the mass with their weapons. A green-eyed man swung his golden scythe and instantly dropped one of Tern's men. Tern cried in rage. His sword slashed the green-eyed man, causing him to stumble off the stairs and fall to the floor below.

While Kumpashin rejoined the angels above, I scanned the chaos for Securitie. I couldn't find her. My heart raced as I shot between the stone houses. Not there. I checked the tree line. Nothing.

Sounds of the continuing battle faded as I flew down to the docks. Two beings flickered into view on the last dock. I folded my wings and ran the rest of the way there.

It was Licemah all over again. Protex stood with arms wide and palms out. Securitie hovered in the air just in front of him. Black enérgeia slithered around her body. Soon, it would cover her entirely.

I blasted yellow enérgeia at the black tendrils. It ricocheted into the dark water below. I cried out in desperation and imagined the demon weighed as much as a feather. He only smirked and remained planted on the dock.

What was happening?

I charged down the dock toward him, but one of the tendrils smacked at me before I could get close. A terrible pain dropped me to my knees. I was out of breath. I craned my neck to look up at Securitie. Her pale face trembled as more tendrils constricted her body.

"Should I give her *mercy*, Cair? Should I give her the same *mercy* you gave to Kynd?"

Each of Protex's words trembled with anger. I couldn't respond, couldn't call for the others, couldn't summon the enérgeia to save her...

I shut my eyes. This was it. I was ready to go to God's Country. Securitie would come, too...and we'd see Laff...Cuverr...Zafe...

Protex's words sounded far off. "She was my everything...and you *took* her away from me...'s only fair you die, too..."

He gagged like something was caught in his throat. There was a loud thump as something hit the dock. Protex's sputtering grew louder as the pain slowly left my body. I opened my eyes.

Through my bleary vision, I saw Securitie had fallen right in front of me. Her wings hung over each side of the dock. With her arms folded under her and eyes closed, she looked like she could be meditating. I reached under the disheveled curly hair and touched the side of her cold face. My lip trembled and fresh tears ran down my cheeks.

Protex had fallen to his hands and knees. He tried to crawl forward, towards us. His eyes locked with mine. I saw the desperation and pain behind them, but I didn't care. His body shook as he reached a wobbling arm out to me. Protex finally collapsed on the dock. Then, I saw the snake-hilted sword in his back. The demon's body turned into ash and the night wind blew it out to sea. The sword clattered on the dock.

"It feels so *good* to hold this again," Sage crooned as she picked it up. I pulled my body up over Securitie's.

"Don't worry, Cair, I won't use the Shadow Sword on you tonight."

Sage walked past me and onto the beach. She raised the sword high and screamed to the darkness.

"Shadows, to me!"

A small cloud appeared above her. Eleven, maybe twelve Shadows wailed in the black whirlwind of red eyes and hungry mouths. Sage grinned with satisfaction. She flicked the sword and the Shadow cloud vanished. Then, the demon turned her attention to the kneeling figure before her.

"Why if it isn't *Friend*. Do you have something to say?"

"I offer my allegiance to ya, Sage," Friend whined. "Please, don't do me in!"

Sage sheathed the sword. "All right. I accept your allegiance. Now, let's go."

Friend mumbled wordlessly and disappeared. Sage glanced up the hill. Then, she turned back around. Her yellow eyes took in my beaten figure still crouched over Securitie.

"Until next time, Cair."

She vanished into the salty air.

28

CURSE OF THE BOTO

"Come on, Cair..."

I clung tighter to Securitie's body. Her red curls were wet from my tears.

"You can't do nothing for her now. Here, I gotcha..."

Strong, gentle arms pulled me away from her and into Gentull's burly chest. I broke down and cried like a wounded animal. Gentull's calloused hand stroked the top of my head. Suddenly, his hand tensed.

"Let's get off the dock, shall we?"

I felt the soft sand and knew we were back on the beach. A gust of wind rushed past my face and I heard Gentull cough. His strong arms guided me away from his body. I opened my eyes, then shut them quickly. They fluttered open again to see the white light that had turned the night into day.

The Voice was in His angel form. His radiance lit up the beach and the town. He landed on the dock and crouched over Securitie's body. I knew what was coming so I looked away.

Maybe she didn't die, maybe she's still there...

But when I looked back, her body was gone. I sank to my knees.

The Voice raised His hand. "My humans who have traded Me for those foul abominations, come down!"

Twenty or thirty of the green-eyed men and women floated down the hill, struggling against the invisible force that bound them. They came to rest in the shallows of the dark sea.

"You have slain your brothers and sisters," the Voice continued. Every syllable trembled with anger. "Some of them were fathers and mothers. You *orphaned* their children. I am merciful, but I still require justice. Therefore, you and your children shall be cast into the sea!"

The humans wailed as their skin turned gray and rubbery. Clothing ripped as their bodies bulged. Legs melted into tails and arms flattened into flippers. Ears disappeared. Pointy teeth filled their long mouths.

The Voice dropped His hand. The new creatures dropped into the water, clicking and squealing with their new voices.

"You are now known as the *boto*. Fish will be your food and you will be in terror of the creatures of the deep ocean. Swim away from these shores and find your repentance!"

Dozens of gray forms disappeared below the waves. Several jumped as much as ten feet in the air before sinking back into deeper water. They fled with terrified clicks and squeals. Soon they were gone.

The Voice faced the town and raised His arm a second time. "My humans who have stayed true to Me, I am coming up!"

The light swirled in patterns across His body as He walked by me. Right by me! Why didn't He stop?

Gentull laid his war-hammer down in the sand. "Cair, we should follow Him."

I wiped my eyes on my robe and turned away. My wings unfurled from my back. Instead of going up the hill to the town, I soared east over the treetops.

STONE BIRD

I reached the Garden. Fireflies hovered over the surface of the pond and the water lily glowed like a pearl in the moonlight. I crouched at the water's edge.

Lily. Lily, it's me.

By the Voice, Cair. It's past midnight! What brings you here this late?

Are there any new angels? I pressed. *Have any angels become flowers tonight?*

Silence.

Lily?

I'm sorry, Cair, she answered sadly. *There haven't been any new angels in centuries. What's going on? Cair, wait!*

I ignored her mental pleas as I flew away. I followed the creek until I came to an azalea, a caladium, a peony and a rose clustered together on the bank. I'd seen them before.

Next, I found the two daffodils near the eight-foot-tall morning glories. Nothing new.

I checked the tree line, the open clearing, even under the red-leafed banana leaves where the giant butterflies stayed at night. No sign of any new flowers.

I sat down in the open clearing and stared off into the dark trees. The grass felt cool beneath my hands. I pulled up a clump of it and threw it in the air. The wind scattered the grass. My chin rested on my knees while I rocked back and forth in agitation.

A familiar screech made me look up. A golden bird flew north across the black sky. It was Jolene the alicanto bird! She knew Securitie was still alive, knew where she was, could take me to her...

"Jolene! *Jolene*!" I cried, taking to the sky once more. "Wait for me, Jolene!"

She screeched again and continued her flight. She was going to lead me to Securitie, who'd be waiting with gold for Jolene. Then, after a good joke, the three of us would return to Tern's town.

Yes, I told myself. *That's what'll happen.*

Now snow glistened on the forest beneath us. Jolene gained height as the Glacier Mountains came into view. She let out another screech and plunged into the ghostly clouds. I stopped by one and felt the chill as it rolled by.

"Jolene!" I shouted into the cloud bank. No answer. That was fine, because I knew where she was going. I adjusted my course towards the valley between the westernmost peaks.

I heard the roaring waterfalls. Pre-dawn mist rose from the basin and shrouded the stone buildings. I made my way through the silent city. Securitie would be here at our old home. An unpleasant feeling gnawed at me, but I pushed it away. She *was* here.

I glided over the open Temple roof. I passed over the spot where Securitie and I sat many years ago. That silly angel and her jokes about worms! My wings carried me to the quarters. The front staircase had been collapsed by Kynd during the Battle of Licemah. I retracted my wings and walked down the drafty hallway. Securitie's room was down here on the bottom floor.

I came through her doorway only to find an empty room. Her chair lay sideways on the floor. The cotton blanket bunched up near the bed's bottom, like some animal had been sleeping in it. All her scrolls, quills and ink bottles had been taken away when the Voice made us leave.

The Voice, I thought bitterly. *He should know why she's not here.*

A soft trill came from the windowsill. Jolene was perching there, gazing at me with her golden eyes.

"There you are!" I cried with relief. "Jolene, where is she? Where's Securitie?"

She lowered her head.

"Where is she? Tell me where she is!"

The alicanto blinked. A single tear escaped her eye. She spread her wings to their full span. She screeched again, the sound full of loneliness and grief. Her body glowed with a yellow light that pierced the mist. Then, the screech ended and the light dimmed.

Jolene had become a part of the room. The bird wasn't even breathing. She stood still like a statue. She was now the same gray as the floor and the walls; all of her lush color had disappeared. Except from her eyes. They stayed open in an eternal golden gaze.

I touched her. Her entire body was as hard as stone.

As the first rays of the morning sun pushed through the mist, that unpleasant feeling finally broke through my hope. Jolene hadn't come to lead me to Securitie. She came because she already knew Securitie had died. The Garden confirmed it: Securitie's soul had passed on to God's Country.

I fell to the floor, sobbing, with my arms around the statue's feet.

30

GOD'S COUNTRY

The morning looked down on the town by the sea. Men and angels helped each other fit doors on every doorway. The bodies of the fallen were hauled into the forest for burial. Smells of eggs and sausage came from the town firepit. The surviving women were feeding their hungry children. A few waved at me as I walked by, but I ignored them as I headed for the tallest building.

A jumble of voices grew steadily louder with each step I took up the stairs. I reached the top to find Tern and Gard sitting together on a long bench. They faced the swirling, white ball that was the Voice.

"Tern, son of Manson," the Voice rumbled. "Because of faithfulness, I promise to make your town the greatest city of Blueshade. You are as faithful to Me as your father before you."

Tern bowed his head. Gard saw me and raised his hand in greeting.

"Ah, Cair, welcome back…"

"Don't you 'ah, Cair' me!"

The words came out in force and Gard raised his eyebrows. I marched right up to him and jabbed my finger at his chest.

"She's dead, Gard! Securitie is dead!"

"She is among several who were slain in last night's confrontation. I understand your grief…"

"No, you don't!" I snapped at him and shook my finger in his face. "You don't understand any…"

Clouds suddenly rolled across the rising sun. I fell silent as the Voice spoke, His words firm and strong. "Gard and Tern, continue your future plans for this town. I will speak with Cair."

The sea, the people, the entire town disappeared. I closed my eyes against a light so bright that I could feel it through my eyelids. Air rushed all around me, whooshing like it blew through a cavern mouth. My feet *felt* as if they stood on solid ground, but I wasn't sure. Gradually, the color darkened and I opened my eyes. The world was white, but not the glaring, searing white anymore.

The Voice spoke. His words shook me like an earthquake.

Little one, why have you treated your brother with such contempt?

I stumbled and caught myself before falling. I was in an empty, white space that stretched high above me. The powerful presence of the Voice filled every corner of this wide, unknown place. My legs trembled; I knew that His majestic power could crush me in an instant.

Do not have an unhealthy fear of My wrath, He rumbled as if reading my mind. *If you are angry with Me, find the root cause of your anger. Again, why have you treated your brother with such contempt?*

How can Gard be so calm after last night? I answered. *Securitie is dead, more humans are dead and he doesn't shed a tear!*

Gard has shed many tears. While you dealt with grief in your own way, Gard dealt with it in his. What concerns Me now is you. Tell me your worries. I will listen.

His calm invitation only frustrated me. I looked around for His ball of light or His angel form. Any visible part of Him to target my anger on.

Why did You curse those humans? You could've destroyed the Shadows just like You've done before. Then, Protex and Sage wouldn't have gotten involved, and Securitie would still be alive!

The whooshing winds died down. Was the Voice considering my words? I didn't care.

Sage and the other demons are still out there in the world! God, why don't You destroy them? Surely, You see all the horrible things they're doing to Blueshade! How could You offer redemption to any of them? They don't deserve it!

Suddenly, I was looking at a brown-haired, freckle-faced angel across the space. She hurled all of her pain at me through her words.

They don't deserve it! She yelled and balled up her fists. *They keep hurting us and the humans through deception and outright bloodshed! And what do You do? You just sit up there in God's Country and pop down here when You feel like it!*

Oh, the frustration in her voice, the hurt in her eyes. If she could only see herself the way I did...

And then I was back in the wide space. The Voice spoke again.

Put aside your bitterness. Did you not just see for yourself how I care about you? I know the despair in your soul and the depth of your weeping each time someone you love is taken from you. Your accusations are misplaced, little one. I am not upset by the words you have spoken. I am sympathetic to your pain because I feel it as well...

An invisible giant hand pushed against my back and held me to the unseen floor. Like a lion had his claws in me and was pulling them out one at a time.

Do not be fearful as I rebuke you, because I discipline those I love. I want to know how you feel, not so I can reprimand you, but so I can help you understand My ways. Examine your memories and compare them to your feelings now.

Even under the heavy pressure of His hand, I could see my most precious memories. The triumphant smile on Gard's face when he won the race back to Licemah. The time I listened to Lily's singing for half a day. Securitie's unashamed laughter ringing through the mountain air. And Hurr's smiling face as we plummeted side by side towards the basin beneath us...

All these memories shone like jewels against the emotions that now raged inside me. They burned holes in the anger that had consumed me. I realized that the anger only masked the pain buried under it.

Surrender this burden to Me, Cair. Let Me take it from you.

I felt the weight shift onto shoulders of Someone stronger than me. Through the transfer, I had a glimpse of His love for me. Strong. Fierce. Compassionate. Forgiving. Then, I saw His love stretching beyond me and reaching across all of Blueshade. The Voice loved everything He had created. He mourned for the beings lost to the Void. He yearned for all living creatures to walk in His ways and involved Himself daily in their lives. The Voice longed to bring them all into God's Country. And suddenly His monument, the one built in Licemah centuries ago, made sense to me.

I have great patience, but it is not unlimited. For every sin committed against Me and their fellows, My judgement draws closer. Only their repentance and My sacrifice will stay My wrath.

The weight lifted from my back. It took away my rage. Something wet dripped on my head and I felt the familiar sensation of compassion bringing coolness and calm. The liquid ran down my face as I looked straight ahead at a black line spreading across the white space. That part of the space peeled forward. A million things escaped from the place beyond. A vague shoreline beside a body of water. Wonderful fragrances I've never smelled before. And singing, beautiful singing, of humans, yarl and angels. No words, but a melody which reminded me of a time when the world was new.

I wasn't sure how long I stood there, basking in the experience. But a gentle nudge brought me out of it. The Voice was next to me in His angel form. The hard words I'd said to Him came back in a rush and I bowed before Him.

God, forgive me. I was in pain and I lashed out in anger. I will make it right.

Your repentance reveals your heart, He answered. He grabbed my arm and helped me rise again. *But only My sacrifice can make it right.*

This was the second time He mentioned sacrifice. What did He mean?

You are my beloved child, Cair, the Voice continued. *There is a task waiting for you in Blueshade should you choose to return.*

Choose to return?

You have a choice. You can return to Blueshade and continue your guardianship over mankind. Or you can enter God's Country where you will find eternal rest.

31

COMPASSION

"Cair? What are you...*oof!*"

Gard stumbled backwards as I threw my arms around him.

"I'm sorry," I whispered in his ear. "I shouldn't have treated you that way."

He relaxed his shoulders and awkwardly patted me on the head. I let him go. We stood on the docks of Tern's town. It was a gray mid-morning; the sun tried to peek through the clouds. Cawing seagulls fought the winds as they flew over the churning waves. For a moment, the humans who'd been changed into *boto* crossed my mind. What would become of them in the deep sea?

"You have my forgiveness, Cair," Gard said. The wooden boards creaked as we walked towards the beach. "Why did you choose to come back?"

"Because of them."

I waved at the two humans who fished in the shallows. As one of them waved back, an enormous tug nearly jerked the fishing pole out of his hands. He gripped the pole with both hands and yelled with delight. His companion grabbed around his waist. Together they pulled the fifty-pound redfish to shore.

"These humans," I continued as we trudged up the hill. "If Protex had destroyed me, I wouldn't be around to help them."

"True," Gard agreed. "You already have an established relationship with the four children of Manson. I believe them and their children will be critical to the rest."

As we crested the hill, I saw mounds of dirt at the edge of the forest. Tern knelt by one of them. He clutched his ten-year old daughter who sobbed on his shoulder. The sight awakened the compassion inside of me. It must've shown on my face because Gard nudged me in their direction.

"Tern lost his wife in the attack last night," Gard said softly. "And Yaz her mother."

He remained on the path while I approached the mounds. The girl saw me first and tugged on her father's sleeve. Tern looked up and I saw the same grief in his eyes that I was all too familiar with. I knelt down next to the humans.

"Tern, I'm sorry for my actions this morning," I told him. "I, too, I-lost..."

My voice broke as the grief washed over me anew. Hot tears stung my cheeks. Little hands stroked my hair. Yaz's brown eyes gazed at me through the mess of her dark curls. I saw sadness and strength mingled together in them. She had survived something no child should ever have to go through.

Tern sniffled. He squeezed Yaz as if he'd never let her go again. My wings folded around them, giving them us privacy as our tears fell.

I spent the rest of the day with Tern and Yaz. Fifteen people had been slain by the Shadow-led humans. Tern presided over a public funeral that afternoon. Wooly blue mistflowers had been gathered from the forest eaves and placed on top of the mounds. The community chose to dress in black-dyed garments to honor their dead. They circled the mounds as Tern read from his Sacred Book. Yaz cried into my chest and I stroked her hair. Our trembling voices sang "The Death Song". Mine broke halfway through it.

Tern held an early supper in the unfinished building. That meal showed me the power of community. Tragedy had ripped Tern's town apart. But hope was sewing it back together. When the meal ended, I left Yaz in the company of the older women. I had reached the edge of town when she caught up to me. She tossed her hair and put a hand on her left hip.

"Angel, where are you going? Are you *leaving*?"

"For a little while," I explained to her. "There are some things I need to do for the Voice. But don't be scared. You can talk to Him anytime when you use the Link. He will listen to you."

Yaz scrunched up her nose. "He will?"

"He will," I echoed. "Look after your father while I'm away. Can you do that?"

She removed her hand from her hip. It was funny, how small she was, yet she still tried to look bigger. "Mmhmm. Promise you'll come back?"

I raised my hand and summoned a flash of enérgeia. The yellow light swirled around the girl's body. A smile lit up her face and she giggled as she tried to touch it. The light disappeared. I returned her smile as I unfolded my wings.
"I promise."

GOING FORWARD

I rejoined Gard that night. We met at the mouth of the Frost River. Further upstream was Gavin's community. Across the black ocean was Miller and Deanna's home on Bacaniber Island. And west up the coast was Tern's little town.

Our white robes billowed in the night wind.

"How are you, Cair?" Gard asked after a while.

"Better. It's easier to think without Protex in my head."

"Even though he is dead, that demon still did considerable damage. He led humans into rebellion and fed the green shade inside them. He taught them how to steal and how to kill each other. Nonetheless, the humans are answering the call the Voice has given them. The tiny communities are growing into towns, which will grow into cities.

Tern is a strong leader. What do you think of his daughter?"

"She survived the Shadow attack," I said. "I think the people will want her to lead when Tern dies. The horrors they faced will strengthen their bonds."

"Very good. Mankind may have a third realm soon."

"Are you thinking about being its Guardian Angel?"

"Me?" Gard chuckled as if the question amused him. "Well, I *have* thought about it since the last time you asked me. I would prefer to travel from realm to realm, and continent to continent. This way I can aid *all* realms of men."

He gazed out over the ocean as if he could see the other continents. Then he sighed.

"To answer your question, Cair, *I* will not be the Guardian Angel of this new realm. Kumpashin would. He has talked about it for some time."

"As long as there aren't any gigantic insects there."

"Before Kumpashin accepts his new title, he wants to help us on our next mission."

An image of Sage appeared in my head. She wielded the twin-snaked sword that controlled the Shadows above her.

"We're going to find the Shadow Sword, aren't we?"

Gard nodded. "That sword must be destroyed. Hopefully, the Shadows will be destroyed as well."

"Do you know where to find her?"

"I have an idea."

"That's one thing you're never short of."

He gave me a confused look. I held my sides and laughed at him. The silliness of my words finally registered and he allowed himself a chuckle or two before shaking his head.

And in my mind's eye, I could see Securitie laughing with us.

About the Author

Clay Ball was born in Tampa, Florida and has always carried that heritage wherever he goes. He has a BA in English and a decent sense of humor. He works as a substitute teacher in Spartanburg County. He plays on his Xbox and in his band. He goes to church and to Chick-Fil-A.

Clay lives in South Carolina with his sweet daughters, his beautiful wife, fuzzy cats and furry dog.

Follow all of his Blueshade stories on:
clayballwrites.wordpress.com

• Cool things you can see on
ClayBallWrites.wordpress.com
• A world map of Blueshade
• A region map of the Mainland
• A city map of Licemah
• Updates, blogs, and more